Sycamore XL

CRAIG A. FALCONER

Sycamore XL

This edition published May 2022

ISBN: 9781541201897

For Anya,
… times four.

Introduction

Like *Sycamore X*, its ten-story predecessor, ***Sycamore XL*** is a companion collection to the two Sycamore novels. This time, there are not ten but twelve brand new stories.

The novels focused on Kurt Jacobs, whose own focus was on the rapid changes taking place on a societal level. This didn't leave much room to explore how The Seed and UltraLenses were affecting the day-to-day lives of ordinary individuals.

That's where *Sycamore X* came in.

Its ten stories, which occurred in the same general timeframe as the novels, focused mainly on new characters and their experiences in Sycamore's brave new world.

Sycamore XL continues in that vein, exploring more points of view while also delving deeper into the lives of previously featured characters. Many characters recur through these stories, so this collection — like the Sycamore series as a whole — is very much intended to be read in order.

People who have read the novels will naturally get a lot more out of the companion collection than people who haven't. In any case, all readers will need a basic understanding of the core tech. Here's a quick rundown/recap:

UltraLenses: Sycamore's groundbreaking augmented reality contact lenses. Powerful and discreet, The UltraLenses can overlay data in a consumer's vision or fully immerse them in vivid virtual surroundings indistinguishable from reality.

The Seed: Sycamore's implantable microchip. Implanted in the consumer's left hand, The Seed turns their palm into a touch-based trackpad. The Seed's computational power and intuitive input method combines with the UltraLenses' flawless display to create the ultimate human-computer interface.

Thanks to a combination of masterful marketing, political corruption, and fortuitous timing, Sycamore's market penetration is near-total. As such, the following stories occur in a world and time in which it's safe to assume that everyone is Seeded and everyone is wearing Lenses.

Welcome to Sycamore…
enjoy the view.

ONE

Scott

A relaxed and almost-human voice rang through Scott Richter's in-earphones as his Seed's text-to-voice technology relayed a new message from his friend Miles.

"Limo be there soon, hope you ready," it said, semi-successfully attaching a natural-sounding inflection and cadence to the lazily typed message.

"I will be," Scott said out loud. His Seed converted this spoken response to text and sent it to Miles, providing the original sender with a reply in the same format as their first message as it always did unless explicitly instructed otherwise.

A few minutes later, Scott was ready. He knew nothing of what Miles had planned for the evening but knew he was in safe hands; if Scott's proved anything like the previous two bachelor parties Miles had organised, the whole group had a memorable night ahead of them.

Scott pulled his blinds to the side and looked out of the window. There was no limo outside. He waited for a few minutes, quietly wondering whether making him wait was the first part of the evening's entertainment for the rest of the group.

After a long five minutes, Scott gestured into his left palm to send Miles a text: "How soon is soon? I'm ready."

A one-word error message then filled most of Scott's vista: "UNDELIVERED."

The uppercase text was bold and red, its physical appearance as ominous as its very presence. Of however many thousand messages Scott had sent through his Forest profile's fully integrated interface, none had ever been undelivered.

Something was wrong.

As the unwelcome thought crossed Scott's mind that something might have happened to Miles which rendered him unreachable — something from a very short list of possibilities, none of which bore thinking about — he hurriedly tried to initiate a voice call.

"ACTION UNAVAILABLE."

One by one, Scott then tried to call the other guys who were with Miles. For each, the action was unavailable.

Scott took a deep breath and attempted to reason with his own fears, the conscious part of his mind insisting that the communications breakdown was almost certainly a problem at his end and that the limo they were all inside was almost certainly still safely approaching his home.

"Full system check," Scott said as calmly as he could.

Nothing happened.

"I said: full system check."

Though there was still no pop-up, this time something *did* happen. Something worse.

Much worse.

~

"You're an interesting man, Scott Richter," an unfamiliar voice said. This puzzling statement sounded so jerky and inelegant that Scott could only assume the voice was deliberately robotic. The delivery was almost spasmodic, reminding him of the first text-to-voice software he'd ever encountered way back in 2006.

"What the hell is this?" Scott asked, not even sure who or what he was talking to.

"Just business," the voice said after a brief two-second delay. "Nothing personal."

"Disable text-to-voice," Scott ordered, speaking to his Seed's voice-controlled preferences menu. "Block all chat requests and messages from unknown senders. Close all open conversations."

After another two seconds, the robotic voice chuckled fiendishly. "Scott Richter… what gave you the idea that this was a conversation? This is me telling you what you're going to do and you doing it."

"Lock down Forest and quarantine all user data," Scott barked, urging his Seed to shut everything down before…

Before…

Scott didn't even know what he was trying to stop; he just knew that he had to try.

"Poor Scott Richter," the voice replied teasingly. "He still doesn't get it! Here's how it is, Scott… everything already *is* locked down. If you don't believe me, just try to report a security breach to the SycaSure team."

When Scott clicked to open his Seed's main menu, every single option — including SycaSure — was greyed out.

"Who are you?" Scott asked, his voice shaking with the painful realisation that his entire Sycamore account had somehow been compromised.

"We'll get to that," the gloating robotic voice replied after the now customary two-second delay. "For now, let's take care of that menu screen, why don't we?"

Scott watched helplessly as every greyed-out option disappeared, replaced by a countdown timer which stood at just under four minutes. The background, previously a semi-transparent blue wash, then became fully immersive and transformed into a collage of images.

There were pictures of Scott's parents, pictures of his nieces, pictures of his fiancée. Each of these images was a snapshot from Scott's Relive timeline; a frame from his private vista recordings, which no one outside of Sycamore and its carefully selected partners were ever supposed to have access to.

Unable to click out of this menu, Scott could only watch the time tick down. "What the hell is going on?" he demanded. "What happens when it reaches zero?"

"You don't want it to reach zero," the robotic voice replied.

Below the timer, now nearing three minutes, a new button appeared. It displayed a so-called *Freedom Fee* which Scott quite simply couldn't afford to pay. "I'm not paying a ransom," he said, pretending to be taking such a stance by choice.

"I don't think you're grasping this, Scott. I have *everything*. I've been in your account for five days, and I've isolated all of the things you *really* don't want anyone to see."

"There's nothing I don't want anyone to see," Scott said, confident in the words.

After the customary two-second delay, a video played in full immersion. "I wonder what your fiancée would say about this?"

"Nicole knows where we went," Scott said as the inside of a seedy-looking bar filled his vista. It struck him as even dingier now than it had then, doubtless because his eyes and mind weren't blurred by alcohol as they had been when Miles took him and the rest of the guys there for another friend's bachelor party just six weeks earlier. "There's nothing she doesn't know."

The footage continued unbroken by a reply for longer than two seconds; Scott assumed that whoever was behind the voice would be scrambling to find something else now that the "evidence" he was supposed to be scared of had been revealed as reassuringly innocuous. He forgot how much he hated the voice until it returned:

"Whatever you say, Scott. But I wonder what your employer would have to say about *this*?"

A briefer snippet of footage then played, again from Scott's first-person point of view. This time he was sober and at work, busy retelling a joke during his lunch break: "*How many feminists does it take to change a lightbulb?*"

"That wasn't even a bad joke!" Scott snapped defensively before his recorded self reached the punchline.

"*Really*?" the voice said, unnaturally elongating the word for awkward robotic emphasis. "In *this* social climate?"

A barrage of news headlines and viral Forest posts then scrolled across Scott's vision, reminding him of the countless men — and indeed the handful of women — who had recently been fired from their respective jobs having been caught making comments deemed inappropriate in one way or another.

The voice went on: "And as for *this* one..."

Scott then cringed as he watched his colleague one-upping the feminism gag with a less easily defended joke about a sexually transmitted disease and heard himself laughing along.

"Participating in exclusionary humour like this on company property is grounds for dismissal and you know it," the voice prodded.

Scott knew it was right. "But you can't share the footage without revealing yourself," he said, desperately changing his tone. "And then you would go to jail. Hacking anything to do with Sycamore means jail time, no exceptions."

"I'm in control of your whole account, Scott. When are you going to understand that? Any footage I share, any messages I send... everything will look like it's coming from you."

"I'm not paying you," Scott said defiantly. "If I pay you once, you'll come back for more. That's how extortion works. And how do I know you wouldn't share the footage even if I paid?"

"Fine, don't pay. But make sure to enjoy your night, because there won't be too many more parties when you're unemployed. There won't be much of anything. What do you think your fiancée will have to say about *that*? How will you afford to care for the twins she's carrying?"

The defiance faded from Scott's voice. "I don't even *have* that much money. My credit is almost maxed out."

"Borrow it," the voice suggested.

Scott then saw his Borrow menu appear in his vision, with Miles already highlighted as his recommended lender and the desired amount — more than Scott was comfortable asking for — already filled in on the form. Miles had a good job and had lent non-trivial amounts to several of his friends in recent weeks, so Scott wasn't surprised to see him as the top recommendation.

"There's no link," Scott said.

"I'll lift the communications block so you can contact your recommended lender."

Scott saw the big round Borrow button appear beside the picture of Miles. He pressed it.

"Oh, and Scott? Don't say why you need it. Understood?"

"Whatever," Scott said, waiting for Miles to respond.

"REQUEST AUTOMATICALLY ACCEPTED [BELOW LENDER'S CONFIRMATION THRESHOLD FOR CURRENT FRIEND LEVEL]."

Scott was as relieved as he was surprised. He and Miles were Level One friends — the closest kind — but he still hadn't expected Miles to have his account set up to automatically lend such a large sum without so much as an explanation. The positive credit balance in the corner of Scott's screen was the highest he'd ever seen, but it wouldn't last long.

The countdown timer returned to Scott's vision, now at just twenty seconds.

"Good timing," the voice said. "You should really press it, though…"

Scott gritted his teeth and pressed the button to execute the credit transfer from his compromised Sycamore account to the soulless hacker. He held hope of being reimbursed by Sycamore given that he had been assured his account was unhackable, but right now he was only concerned about appeasing the hacker for the sake of protecting his own job.

"Why hasn't it stopped?" Scott said as the timer reached fifteen seconds.

"You were right," the voice said.

Ten seconds.

"I *am* going to share it anyway. Goodbye, Scott. Thanks for the money."

"No!" Scott shouted.

Five seconds.

"No!"

Three seconds.

"No!"

One second.

And then, as the timer hit zero and the hacked menu screen vanished from Scott's vision, his bedroom door burst open and four of his closest friends bundled through.

"Surprise!" Miles yelled, grinning like only he could. "Man... the look on your face!"

"Wait... what?"

"Yeah," Miles said, nodding enthusiastically. "We pranked you *hard*."

Too relieved to be angry, Scott covered his face with his hands and laughed along with everyone else. "But *how*?" he asked when the laughter died down. "How the hell did you get inside my account?"

"We didn't," Miles said. Though he said we, he was the only one talking and Scott fully expected it had been solely his idea. "There's this premium app. It's still in beta — invite only — but I know a guy. It's called Pranksom. You know, like ransom and prank... Pranksom? It's built on the same tech as the apps employers use for background checks, when they scan your history for un-PC comments and other liabilities. But instead of that, Pranksom has some fun with it."

"So *none* of it was real? What about the voice that was replying to everything I said? And what about the money I borrowed from you?"

Miles quickly checked his account. "You didn't borrow

money from me," he said, smiling again after a brief moment of concern. "And the voice is just AI. The guy said it might take a few seconds to make sense of your responses but that you probably wouldn't notice. What was the stuff it was holding over you, anyway?"

"That 'bar' you took us to for Sam's party," Scott said, air-quoting the word bar. "It was going to show Nicole until I said she already knew. Then it was footage of me telling Chris from work that stupid feminism joke."

"That's not even a bad joke," Miles laughed.

Scott was laughing too. "That's what I said! So then it showed me laughing along to another joke Chris told. And we were at work, so obviously it was on company property."

"What was the joke?" Miles asked, eyes lighting up since he knew it had to be good.

"Okay. There's this guy who works in a hospital, right? And one of the patients is—"

One of Scott's previously silent friends, the recently married Sam, cut him off. "I don't want to hear this," he said.

"Why?" Miles asked him, annoyed by the interruption.

"Because the system flagged Scott laughing at this joke as an incriminating event. I don't want that on *my* record."

"It wasn't real," Scott said. "Were you not listening to a word Miles just said? The whole app is a prank."

"Are *you* not listening to what *I'm* saying?" Sam replied. "Something in Sycamore's system flagged that joke as inappropriate. And if you want to talk about what Miles just said, he said that employers use the same tech. I don't want to lose out on a job because he wants to hear your stupid doctor joke."

"Wait," another friend chimed in, looking at Miles. "If it flagged the bar from Sam's party, it's sure as hell going to flag the place you're taking Scott tonigh—"

"Shut up!" Miles snapped. "That's supposed to be a surprise."

Sam, already too worried about his future employment opportunities to listen to a joke, was equally concerned by this new point. “I’m not going anywhere that’s going to get flagged.”

“Jesus,” Miles said. “Is this who we are now? The guys who are scared to tell jokes and have fun in case a computer tells on us?”

No one said anything.

“Scott,” Miles prodded. “It’s your night. Tell Buzz Killington over here that you want to have some fun.”

Torn between Sam and Miles, Scott hesitated. “I guess we could have fun without getting flagged.”

“It flags when you get drunk,” Miles said, shrugging. “So I guess that means we’re all going to be on water all night, right?” he added sarcastically.

“Seriously?” the fourth of Scott’s friends interjected. “It knows when you’re drunk? And that shows up in the employer scan thing, too?”

“I’d say we could play Scrabble,” Miles said, “but one of you princesses might accidentally spell a naughty word.”

Again, no one said anything.

“The limo’s waiting,” Miles said firmly, sandwiching the silence. “We have to go *somewhere*.”

“We’re not going *there*,” Sam replied. The others who knew the original plan nodded in agreement.

Miles conceded. As the others walked outside, he turned to Scott. “It was just a stupid prank,” he sighed. “I didn’t want to ruin your night.”

“I know, man,” Scott said. “But at least now we know not to do anything that could get us in trouble.”

Miles walked away, shaking his head as he mourned his night of intricately planned trouble that would never come to pass.

TWO

Dr McGill

"Tell him I'll be ready in a few minutes," Dr McGill said, sighing the words out in reply to the message that his next patient was waiting outside.

It had been like this all week — non-stop — with a seemingly endless line of school-age children and their Sycamore-related issues. Dr McGill had been quietly advised against using the term "Sycamore-*induced*" and even the word "problems" in any of his formal assessments. "Sycamore-related issues" struck him as sounding like something more worthy of a call to tech support than a visit to a child psychologist, but he was far too close to the promised land of retirement to consider making any waves over these admittedly deplorable corporate intrusions.

The relevant memo from above had gone so far as to strongly urge against any direct references to Sycamore whatsoever, arguing that the kind of issues being reported had been around since children first had 24/7 internet access via the phones in their pockets.

Dr McGill accepted that this was true to a point, but the severity of the issues he was seeing now — not to mention the frequency with which he was seeing them — made clear that

Sycamore's recently released Seed had changed the lives of schoolchildren at least as much as it had changed everyone else's. Most patients still fell into one of the same two broad groups as those with pre-Sycamore digital difficulties, but the symptoms of both selfie-obsessed narcissism and bullying victimhood were now more pronounced than ever before.

The printed notes on Dr McGill's desk told him that his next patient's visit had more to do with bullying than narcissism. The patient, a 14-year-old boy, had been subject to incessant mocking for several days following his mother's accidental sharing of a highly embarrassing family incident. As was so often the case in such instances, no adults noticed or intervened until the victim reached his breaking point. The patient snapped, lashing out at his chief tormentor so violently that the fight left one participant in hospital and the other in a psychologist's office for a mandatory evaluation.

Dr McGill skimmed through the notes; by now, such a story was familiar enough. This particular case had a humiliatingly intimate element at its core, as did so many, but it was an unusual one in that the party whose private footage had gone public was the patient's father rather than the patient himself. The violent reaction of the male bullying victim was more typical and had come to be expected. Of the patients Dr McGill saw, the boys tended to snap more suddenly and more violently than the girls. They also seemed far more likely to express their pain and frustration externally, injuring others rather than themselves. He didn't doubt that the nature of the bullying had as much to do with these generalised differences as anything innate, given that male patients usually reported being openly goaded into lashing out while most of the girls reported more insidious exclusion by their judgemental classmates.

Having been the epicentre of another recent incident regarding a slightly older girl, the name of the patient's school was familiar to Dr McGill. The boy's teacher, whose name also rung a bell, described him as "attentive and well-mannered" and insisted there had been no prior incidents of concern. To Dr McGill, it all looked like a fairly straightforward case of a tormentor pushing his victim too far and paying the price. He expected to sign off on the patient's return to school within a few minutes.

"Send him in," Dr McGill spoke into his intercom.

A few seconds later, the door swung open.

~

Dr McGill stood to greet his patient, who entered alone.

The boy looked around the room. He took it all in: the teddy bears on the wooden bookcase; the smiling sunshine painted on the wall; the waist-high dollhouse that dominated one corner. His expression betrayed the anger and frustration he felt at having to go through with this in such a childishly decorated room, but he managed to keep quiet. Just as Dr McGill wanted to get through the next few months without making any waves, his latest patient wanted to get through the next few minutes without any unnecessary difficulties.

Eventually, the boy sat in the chair opposite Dr McGill's. The room's other free chairs, both positioned near the dollhouse, were clearly intended for much smaller children.

"Most of my patients are a lot younger than you," Dr McGill said, reading the boy's discomfort with his surroundings. "Well, they *used* to be. A lot of kids your age are having… uh, *issues*, with all this new technology."

"I'm not a kid."

"Let's start again," Dr McGill said, forcing a warm smile. "My name is—"

"Norman Barrett McGill," the boy said.

Dr McGill's eyes narrowed. "How did you—"

"It's written in the air beside your head."

"Oh… of course. Now, can you confirm your full name and age for me, David? I know that's written in the air beside *your* head, but I need to be sure it's correct. David Brown. 14 years old. Yes?"

"Obviously," David said. "The system doesn't make mistakes."

"Is that so?"

David shrugged. "Unless you know something I don't?"

"I know about the data sharing mishap that landed you in this—"

"That wasn't the system's mistake," David interrupted. "The system doesn't *make* mistakes."

"Let's take a step back and focus more on what happened at school," Dr McGill suggested, changing tack. "Why do you think you're here, David?"

Half-heartedly fighting a grin, David answered: "Well, Dr McGill, I guess I'd have to say I'm here because Cameron Black can't take a punch."

Dr McGill almost broke into a smile of his own at David's unexpected reply. "Okay… maybe we'll come back to that. Let's start with the catalyst. You learned of the Everstrong mishap only when the data was made public, correct? And please, call me Norman."

Put at ease by the man's relaxed tone and friendly expression, David recounted the whole story from the beginning. He told Norman about the ad placement that Everstrong Fidelity Check targeted to his mother and about everything that came next: After the Everstrong app had emptied her credit balance and provided first-person video evidence of her husband's dalliance, Helen Brown accepted the app's offer of letting him know that he'd been caught. But then, to Helen's dismay, the app delivered its *gotcha* by posting the entirety of its investigative file publicly on his Forest profile.

The embarrassment began instantly for everyone involved. But David, who had to face a classroom full of weakness-sniffing teenagers, bore the brunt of the fallout.

As David ran through the whole story while Norman

nodded every now and again, the boy noticed that the doctor was scribbling notes into his palm.

"Go on," Norman said when David paused.

David's gaze fell on Norman's desk. More precisely, it fell on the doctor's notepad and pen. "Why do you have a pen?" he asked.

"For taking notes," Norman replied, without thinking anything of the question.

David shifted in his seat. "But you're taking notes in your palm."

"Uh..."

"Wait," David said, his tone changing. "You were doing something else. You weren't listening."

"Of course I was listen—"

"I know how much my dad is having to pay for this crap, and you can't even listen to me for five minutes? I mean, he's an asshole and he deserves to pay for what he did... but *you* don't deserve anything from him. You're not even doing your job!"

"Now, David..."

"Don't '*now, David*' me, you money-grabbing rat."

"Excuse me?" Norman said, affronted by the child's insolence. "How do you think your parents would feel about you talking to me this way?"

But this time it was David whose eyes glazed over. This time it was David who gestured into the palm of his Seed hand. After using his SycaStats trial to see what Norman had really been doing while pretending to listen, David scanned the man's public Forest data. "So your sister is a real psychiatrist?" he asked rhetorically, his still distant eyes widening as he read her details. "And she's worked with the CIA? Wow. *And* her taxable income is 63% higher than yours. That must sting, right?"

Norman said nothing.

David Brown was angry at Sycamore, angry at Everstrong,

angry at his father, and angry at the world. Norman McGill had picked the wrong day to get on his bad side.

"So let me get this straight," David said, taking uncharacteristic glee at the doctor's evident unease. "While your little sister has been making bank and catching bad guys, you've been sitting here in a room full of stuffed animals and finger paintings? How do you think *your* parents would have felt about *that*?"

"This is important work," Norman snapped. "The well-being of children is—"

"Your Sincerity rating is nineteen points lower than your Embarrassment rating right now," David interrupted, having activated his free trial of the all-seeing Reader app at the same time as his SycaStats trial. "And we both know that the system doesn't make mistakes."

"Get out of my office," Norman said as calmly as he could.

"Sign my form," David said, sliding it across the desk.

"Get out."

David rose from his seat. "And to think you were just three months from retirement," he said as he reached for the form. "Sure would be a shame if someone found evidence of professional misconduct. Let's say, I dunno, betting on greyhounds when you're supposed to be helping a vulnerable child?"

Norman put his hand on the form before David could take it. "Are you threatening me?"

David stepped back and shrugged. "Depends. Are you signing the form?"

Four tense seconds later, Norman relented. He handed David the signed form. "Now get out."

"Thanks," David said, "but not quite yet." He sat back down.

"What the hell are you doing?"

"You're going to refund my dad's payment and tell the school board I should never have had to come here."

Norman scoffed. "I'm not being dictated to by a jumped up thug who thinks he can—"

"Say no more," David said. He rose once more. "Better hope those bets come in, doc, 'cause you're outta here."

Norman sighed. David heard it and stopped at the door. "Fine," the doctor said. "I'll refund the damn payment."

"And I trust you'll make an equal payment to me as a gesture of goodwill? You know, for wasting my afternoon. Don't worry; we'll keep *that* payment between ourselves."

"Not a chance."

"Don't try me," David said.

"Not a *chance*."

"Doc… I'm not bluffing. Aren't psychologists supposed to be good at reading faces or something?"

Norman's gaze intensified.

"Why don't you activate Reader?" David suggested. *"It'll* tell you that I'm serious. By the way, how does it feel to have forty years of training rendered obsolete by a microchip and a stupid pair of lenses?"

Norman reached for his palm. David assumed he was going to follow the suggestion of activating Reader, but a vista pop-up revealed otherwise:

NEW PAYMENT RECEIVED. VIEW DETAILS?

"Now get the hell—"

"You don't have to say it," David grinned. "I'm going."

David walked along the corridor with a spring in his step, enlivened not only by the money but also what it signified. He had gotten the better of an intelligent adult by using his Seed to spot the man's weakness. David knew more about the functioning of the new technology than most adults — as children his age always did — and he now wondered how else he could use Sycamore's system to his advantage.

He opened the door to the waiting room and tried to wipe the gleeful smile from his face in favour of something more subdued before meeting his mother.

"How did it go?" she asked.

David handed her the signed form. "I can go back to school

and the doctor is going to refund our payment. He said I should never have had to come in."

"But how do you feel?" his mother asked, evidently less concerned about the money than her son's wellbeing.

"Better," David said, his mind still registering the profitable precedent that had just been set. "*Much* better."

THREE

Kate

"It's more than just a blooper reel," Isaiah Amos insisted, doing his best to sell the idea of his latest creation to the individual he had handpicked to host it. "It's the solution to the problem every time someone has said, *"Man, I wish someone had been filming that!"* It's quick, it's light, it's easy, and it's a great way for us to hit those hard-to-reach international markets. *Both* of us."

Kate Pinewood considered the words. But even more than the words, she considered the circumstances in which they were being spoken. In a world where face-to-face meetings were even less necessary than they had been just a few months earlier, Mr Amos had considered this job offer sufficiently important to merit a personal visit to Kate's home.

Even more remarkably, he was alone.

"I know you have dreams, Miss Pinewood," Amos continued, taking note of her softening expression and preparing to seal the deal. "And I know that the career path you had in mind probably didn't include a blooper reel, but—"

"You said it wasn't a blooper reel," Kate interrupted.

Amos grinned; after another long day surrounded by yes men who would sooner follow him into a pit of lava than question his directions, he almost enjoyed Kate's lack of deference.

"I said it's more than *just* a blooper reel," he clarified. "Like how a tiger is more than *just* a cat. But if you really want to split hairs, fine: it's a blooper real. And a tiger is a cat."

Kate said nothing. She hoped Amos would stop there, before he got started on one of his prolonged and often painful analogies. He didn't.

"But, Kate... a tiger is not *just* a cat, is it? Is it not also a streamlined killing machine? An apex predator? A creature perfectly built to dominate all around it?" After this final question, which Kate presumed to be rhetorical, Amos stared at her as though awaiting an answer.

"Listen," she said. "I appreciate you coming all this way to offer me—"

Amos held his hands up. "Say no more." He opened the door and stepped outside.

"Thank you," Kate said, sighing the words in relief that he was taking no for an answer so easily.

"No, thank *you*," Amos replied as he walked down the path towards his waiting car. "It's great to have you on board. We're shooting at 8am tomorrow, 19th floor. Be early."

"But I didn't say yes!"

Amos stopped abruptly halfway between the door and the car. "Kate," he said, gazing back at her and almost whispering despite the distance between them. "There are two kinds of mistakes. Trust me when I tell you that this isn't the kind you get to make twice."

Kate watched Amos step inside the long black car without so much as a backwards glance. It sped off silently, leaving her speechless at the door.

After several minutes spent wondering what had just happened and what might come next, Kate Pinewood navigated into her Seed's Utilities menu and set an alarm for 6am.

~

Fifteen days later, Kate stepped out of an otherwise empty elevator and walked briskly towards her dressing room on Sycamore HQ's 19th floor, all set to film the third episode of *This Week On Sycamore*.

The 19th floor — which lay far above most employees' security clearance and only eight levels below the secretive Treehouse — hosted one of Sycamore's fastest-growing divisions: Sycamore International. And already, not even three weeks into its life, Kate's show was that division's shining light.

"Good morning, Miss Pinewood," said one voice after another. She didn't stop to chat. After a brief rendezvous with her stylist, Kate arrived in the studio to run through her lines and look over the featured clips before filming began.

With the first two episodes of *This Week On Sycamore* each ranking in the SycaStore's top ten most-viewed shows, the near-total market penetration provided by such prominent positioning within Sycamore's Video app had already made Kate a huge star.

Isaiah Amos had been present for the filming of the first show and insisted that the elephant in the room had to be dealt with straight away. That elephant, of course, was Kate Pinewood's highly public outing as an actress posing as a contestant during the Talent Search at which Kurt Jacobs first presented his concept for The Seed. Amos took full responsibility for trying to use Kate as a plant to present the SycaPhone on that fateful night, even going so far as to insist that the show's writers work in a joke at his expense. He had laughed from behind the camera when Kate read it from her autocue:

"For those of you who think you recognise my name or my face… yes, I *am* the girl who Kurt outed as a plant. But I was following orders from Isaiah Amos, and he was just trying to make the world a better place. And really, however stupid his idea to use a plant to pitch the SycaPhone might have been, we all know it wasn't as stupid as the SycaPhone itself! Because seriously... of all the things Kurt Jacobs has done for us, saving us from that monstrosity of a gadget is surely the greatest."

Images of the SycaPhone prototype had then appeared on screen, surrounded by brightly coloured moving annotations and reaction gifs, as was the show's style. This light-hearted opening segment set the tone for *This Week On Sycamore*, and Amos had been glad to see the combination of humorous content and snappy editing strike a particular chord with young viewers.

What pleased Amos most of all was that *This Week On Sycamore* was as popular overseas as it was at home. The show rounded out Sycamore International's roster of offerings, fitting in nicely alongside the international news service and a series of virtual apps which had been designed to give consumers in other countries an opportunity to experience some of what the Seed and UltraLenses had to offer.

Star's Eye View — the app which allowed consumers to experience someone else's life in glorious first-person immersion — had been popular with foreign viewers from the outset. Amos saw Kate Pinewood as a bridge between Sycamore International's news content and Star's Eye View's celebrity-worship; the role at *This Week On Sycamore* was perfect for her.

Officially employed as a SycAmbassador in recognition of the important role she played in putting Sycamore's best foot forward to a global audience, Kate spent her first week in the new job pinching herself to make sure she wasn't dreaming.

Filming for the pilot episode had taken no more than an hour and by the end of the day Kate's face had appeared on millions of televisions around the world, as well as via the UltraLenses of a huge portion of Sycamore's domestic consumer base. Foreign media outlets and reviewers described Kate as "charming", "energetic", and "a perfect fit for a perfect show." Her Forest profile rocketed up the popularity charts. Lucrative ad-placement offers rolled in almost immediately. And best of all, she enjoyed the work.

Having known next to nothing of what to expect before

filming the pilot, Kate was pleasantly surprised by the show's combination of blooper-reel classics and modern takes on public embarrassment. There were rope swings collapsing into rivers, excited dogs tripping their owners, and, of course, brides falling face-first into their wedding cakes. Along with these age-old blunders there was also a snappily edited montage of consumers walking into objects when overly engrossed by their digital content, plus a handful of instances of people thinking they were in the wrong place because the AR street renovations around them were so convincing.

The format seemed like a winner from the start, which was why Kate had been so surprised to hear of a change of direction just minutes before filming the second episode.

Clive, the man who ran the show and reported only to Amos, explained to his team that Sycamore's extensive data analysis had revealed a clear and unignorable pattern: domestic consumers were using the "like" function to show their approval for the most painful and humiliating clips. In an effort to give the people what they wanted, the second episode therefore included many more such clips. Kate argued that the show would work best if viewers were laughing *with* the subjects of the clips rather than laughing *at* them, but Clive was insistent. Kate and the handful of others who shared her view quietly got on with their jobs, hopeful that viewers would soon grow tired of seeing people getting hurt and that the less mean-spirited clips would make a comeback before long.

This hope failed to materialise.

After the second week's data analysis further proved the direct correlation between how painful or degrading a clip was and how many likes it received, the pre-filming production meeting for the third show gave Kate the distinct impression that *This Week On Sycamore* looked set to descend into little more than a humiliation reel.

The most liked clip in the second episode featured a 14-year-old boy named David Brown mercilessly knocking out a tormentor who had been mocking him over an embarrassing

— and highly public — family matter. The punch David delivered was followed by an excited bystander's call of *"Holy balls! That right there is why you don't mess with Dave!"*, which had already become a viral slogan and been featured in several auto-tuned dance tracks. Footage showed the punch from both David's first-person perspective and that of the recipient. Sycamore owned all footage recorded via any pair of Ultra-Lenses, meaning that the fallen boy had no say in whether or not "his" footage could be played.

Kate didn't mind that particular clip too much — it was far from the worst, certainly — but the sheer number of violent clips mentioned in the script for the third episode left her in no doubt that the data analysis team had misinterpreted *why* David's clip had become so popular. It was apparent that instead of factoring in the natural justice element which was inherent to a clip of a bullying victim finally striking back, Clive and whoever else put the show together believed they could replicate the clip's success by filling the upcoming episode with no fewer than four schoolyard knockouts.

Kate bit her lip as she scanned her lines. Some of the one-liners she would have to say while the fights played were bad enough, but her resolve cracked when she reached a section called *No Take-Backs*.

"There's no way I'm saying that," she said to Clive. "This whole *No Take-Backs* thing... I'm not doing any of it."

Clive had anticipated an argument over *No Take-Backs,* his big idea for a compilation of incidents involving consumers who had accidentally posted something private in public and were unable to take it back before the damage was done. Some of the posts and images in question would have to be blurred out to comply with broadcast restrictions in certain countries, but the distraught reactions of the people whose lives had been ruined were to be displayed in all their HD glory. The accompanying comments crossed all kinds of lines for Kate; there was no way she could bring herself to revel in *this* level of misfortune.

"Kate, if you're not willing to do your job then I'll find someone else who is," Clive said. He didn't dislike her, but he did resent the chasmic difference in their incomes. "I mean, there's bound to be at least *one* more blond actress out there who can read."

"*You're* the replaceable one," Kate snapped back. "You really think Mr Amos couldn't find another 53-year-old nobody to stand behind a camera and point it at my face?"

Clive stepped forward. "I take orders from him, you take orders from me. Understood?"

As Kate and Clive engaged in a tense stare-down, each waiting for the other to crack, a gasp from the other side of the studio broke the silence. So sudden and sharp was the gasp, both turned immediately to its source. An imposing man stood at the doorway, visibly irked by the lack of filming going on around him.

"Mr Amos," Clive blurted, rushing over. "I can explain."

"Oh, do feel free," Amos said dryly.

Clive gestured to Kate. "It's her. She won't read her lines."

Amos glanced briefly at Kate then returned his gaze to Clive. "Which lines? Is it something to do with the *No Take-Backs* thing you told me about last night? We can work around—"

"Why does it matter which lines she won't read?" Clive moaned. "She's refusing to do the job she's paid—"

"Get out," Amos boomed at Clive, inches from his face. "Now!"

Silence circled as Clive trudged towards the door. He slipped out quietly, never to return.

"If anyone else is ever planning to take that tone with me, you might as well follow him out the door now," Amos announced, breaking a brief but total silence. He then led Kate into a quiet corner of the studio and, surprising everyone else with a calm manner that bordered on gentleness, asked her what the problem was.

Kate explained her misgivings. "I'll introduce the *No Take-*

Backs segment if I have to," she then said, "but I'm not reading what he's written. It's cruel, and people will link that cruelness to me."

Kate's final point, which revealed that her objections weren't solely moral, made it easier for Amos to empathise. Kindness was alien to him; self-interest he could understand.

"I have an idea," he said. "You want full control of your image, correct? But you also want the full weight of Sycamore behind you?"

She nodded carefully. When he put it like that, it did sound like a lot to ask.

"Then what about Star's Eye View?"

"No."

"You were born for it! Your looks, your charisma, the popularity you've gained from this... put it all together and you'd be up there with Trixilicious at the top of the charts within a week."

Kate said nothing. Trixilicious deserved all the credit in the world for being strong enough to handle her entire life being turned into a non-stop public spectacle, but Kate wasn't mentally equipped for it.

"You're not keen," Amos said, reading her expression aloud. He nodded a few times. "Okay. It was just a suggestion. I want you here, anyway. I *need* you here. But how can we reconcile this? There are going to be more lines you don't like; more *clips* you don't like."

Kate's eyes lit up with a sudden thought. "Not if I replace Clive."

"You want to direct?"

"Or produce," Kate said, not fully aware of the difference. "Or write. Whatever he does. I'm younger than anyone else here, so I'm more in touch with the crowd you're trying to reach. If you give me autonomy over what clips we run and what we say about them, *This Week On Sycamore* will be a better show."

"Autonomy?"

"On this floor," Kate clarified. "Obviously you would have the final say."

Amos liked the sound of Kate's idea even more than he liked the fact that she was bold enough to voice it. "What changes would you make?" he asked. "In general, that is. Today's show has to go ahead exactly as it's written; it's airing in Australia in just over an hour. But don't worry, someone else will read the part you don't want to say."

"The main change is that I should be sitting down," Kate said. "On a sofa, like a chat show. And we should have guests. It should be an hour instead of thirty minutes, and the clips should be more light-hearted and less mean. More fun. That's what people want."

"Really? The voting suggests—"

"The voting is skewed," Kate interjected. "If you actually look at the core engagement metrics, they show that people have shared and re-watched the "laughing *with*" clips way more than the "laughing *at*" clips. Kids are hitting like on the cruel stuff because their friends can see what they've liked and they think it makes them look cool. If likes were anonymous, behaviour would change. We can test that today if you don't believe me."

"You want to completely do away with those kinds of clips? The fights, the bad falls, the attacked-by-a-swarm-of-bees? You want to get rid of *all* of them?"

"If viewers want to see people getting hurt, give them that somewhere else," Kate said. "Find a SycaStar who's willing to injure himself for their amusement. *This Week On Sycamore* is our flagship show; it's the only piece of our content that reaches actual TVs in other countries. It has to be more positive. You don't want people in France tuning in then tuning out in disgust, do you? That's why we should keep it upbeat. Star's Eye View is totally different. It's à la carte, so people can watch exactly what they want and leave everything else. *That's* where you should serve the lowbrow crowd."

Amos let Kate's words sink in, impressed by the depth of

her thinking. "We have this new guy," he said. "Damian Dangerman. He's a SycaStar with a limited audience right now — mainly high-school kids... well, high-school *boys* — but it's growing quickly, in relative terms. He's getting some hype for holding his hand on hot stoves, belly-flopping from rock-faces, you know, real puerile stuff. But it's working. Do you think we should get behind him with some heavy promotion? Perhaps targeted to people who have liked these kinds of clips?"

"Push him to the moon," Kate said, very enthusiastically. "Draw the audience who wants that stuff to him. And since he's only going to be seen by people who have actively sought out his stuff, he can take it as far as he wants. You can make him push the boat *way* out if that's what you want."

Amos nodded and made a mental note to get on this right away. "Now, back to *your* show. Tell me about these guests you have in mind. What *kind* of guests?"

"Viral stars from popular clips," Kate said. "Our first big one could be David Brown, the kid who punched the bully last week."

Amos considered it, looking uncharacteristically agreeable. "And you'll be the one doing the interviewing? By yourself?"

"Unless you don't think I can handle a 14-year-old kid."

Amos clapped his hands together and turned away. "Listen up, everyone: Miss Pinewood is going to be in charge around here from now on. If you don't like that, leave."

No one did.

"Now," Amos continued, "as for today, someone else can do a voiceover for the lines Miss Pinewood doesn't want to read, because there's no time to write around the problem. And speaking of replacements, who in here is capable of taking over the technical side of Clive's job?"

A few enthusiastic hands shot up on the other side of the studio. Amos set off towards them.

"Thank you, Mr Amos," Kate said.

He stopped and looked at her again. "For what?"

"For letting me take over. For believing in me. I feel like this could be the start of something great."

"Of course it will be," Amos said. "I know you know better than to let me down."

"I'll get to work," Kate said, taking the pseudo threat as a challenge, exactly as Amos had hoped she would. He knew he had been right to like her.

Amos once again set off across the studio's wide open space to discuss technical matters with the staff members who had volunteered to fill the void left by Clive's unceremonious departure.

Kate's voice filled the air again seconds later. This time she wasn't speaking to Amos, but rather to someone unseen; someone on the other end of a voice call.

"David Brown?" she said. "This is Kate Pinewood, from *This Week On Sycamore*. How would you like to make some money?"

The words danced in Amos's ears. He looked over his shoulder at Kate and winked.

She would do.

FOUR

Rocco

"Listen up," the guard boomed, preparing to relay a message from his standpoint beside the spartan holding cell.

The eight men inside — twice as many as the cell was intended to hold — all turned to face him, reacting to the first words any of them had heard in days.

"Hearings for the following defendants will commence in five minutes: Steve Keller, Matt Richmond, Rocco Miller. If your name has been announced, step forward now."

"When my lawyer finds out—" one man began to respond. As soon as the sound of his voice registered, the metallic ring around his neck delivered a swift and effective electric shock. The cell fell silent once more.

Rocco Miller stepped forward. The prohibition on speech meant that he didn't know which of his fellow prisoners were which, and the fact that no others had yet stepped forward to join him provided no clues.

Rocco's best estimate placed his incarceration at the five-day mark, but the lack of natural light and the irregularity of meal times — if they could be called meals — made it difficult to be sure. Only two of the other seven men had been present when he was unceremoniously thrown into the cell, and neither them nor any or those who had arrived since had been called for a hearing. Rocco began to assume that the first three men to arrive would be the first three to be called for their hearings, so he expected his two original cellmates to reveal themselves as Steve Keller and Matt Richmond at any moment.

None of the seven men had the kind of appearance Rocco might have expected given his prior exposure to prisoners, which was strictly limited to their portrayal in movies and TV shows. There were no shaved heads in Rocco's holding cell; no visible tattoos; no shoulders broader nor heads taller than his own. Some were several decades older than Rocco, who was the youngest by far at 21. A few looked down on their luck; one in particular was extremely thin, almost alarmingly so, and had eagerly devoured every meagre meal the guards provided as though it was his first and last.

The thin man stepped forward and stood shoulder to shoulder with Rocco, facing the guard.

"And Matt Richmond," the guard said, indirectly identifying the thin man as Steve Keller.

The prisoner who had just been shocked for speaking out of turn then stepped sheepishly forward, revealing himself as Matt Richmond. Matt adjusted the ring around his neck as he eyed the guard with a look of unconcealed hatred.

Rocco momentarily longed for the convenient display of consumer data he would have seen beside Matt's head had he not removed his UltraLenses in a moment of rage and thrown them from a moving vehicle to free himself from their relentless pop-up warnings to stop moving and report to the nearest police officer or Sycamore agent. But he then remembered the guard shining a bright light into his eyes prior to throwing him into the cell and confirming aloud to someone unseen that Rocco had been "fitted with a silencing ring and checked for UltraLenses."

Contrary to Rocco's previous assumption, neither Steve Keller nor Matt Richmond had been in the cell when he arrived. Trying to make sense of the order in which prisoners were being summoned, his new theory was that Steve and

Matt were the only two of his cellmates to have been detained for the same offence he had committed.

This time, he was correct.

As the guard held the door open, Rocco stepped out from his cramped cell. Steve and Matt followed close behind. The guard then ordered the men into a single-file line and removed each of their silencing rings, informing them in no uncertain terms that conversation was still forbidden.

"Walk straight in," the guard said, pointing to a door at the end of the short corridor. "And don't try nothin' funny."

Matt Richmond, still glaring angrily at the guard following his shock moments earlier, led the way. Rocco was next, trailed by Steve Keller's gaunt frame.

"What are you in for?" Steve whispered as they moved out of the guard's earshot and neared the door.

Rocco replied as quietly as he could: "Goddamn Movement Tax."

~

It looked more like a meeting room than the courtroom Rocco had expected, but only one area caught his attention. Over to the right, among a crowd of a dozen or so, he spotted his wife and newborn son.

A trio of guards had already ushered Rocco and his fellow Movement Tax evaders into their seats by the time he noticed his family, so Rocco was unable to greet them with anything more than a mournful look and a quivering lip.

A sixty-something woman with short hair and an impatient expression sat alone at a large desk in front of the defendants. Were they really defendants?, Rocco wondered as the word entered his mind. Nothing about his current situation had been made clear. The first he'd heard of this "hearing" had been just a few minutes earlier, and he didn't know if it would follow the pattern of a criminal trial, some kind of tribunal, a disciplinary hearing, or simply — and hopefully — a stern dressing down.

Rocco couldn't help but think of the imposing woman behind the imposing desk as a judge, whether this was technically correct or otherwise.

"Matt Richmond," she said, speaking the words with a resonance that felt consistent with her general aura of authority. "Would you like to tell me why you're here?"

"I'm not telling you anything without my lawyer present," Matt said, his defiance boosted by the welcome absence of a silencing ring around his neck. He glanced at his brother, who he'd spotted next to the woman with the baby. "Where's Harvey?"

"They wouldn't let him in," the man replied. "Family only."

Rocco didn't know how to feel about this. He was in no position to afford a lawyer, anyway, but did the apparent ban on legal representation mean that this *wasn't* anything as official as a trial, or simply that the hearing's outcome was already determined?

"You don't have to talk," the judge said to Matt, "but I strongly suggest you do. Openness and cooperation may soften my final judgement."

Again, Rocco didn't know what to make of this statement. He didn't like that it confirmed the fact that a judgement about his alleged Movement Tax evasion would soon be made, but he was slightly encouraged to hear that he could potentially cooperate his way into the judge's good books.

"Fine," Matt relented, shifting in his hard plastic chair. "My balance ran out while I was in the middle of a journey. I couldn't pay."

"Having read through your employment records, Mr Richmond, I would expect a man of your means to have a credit allowance even more robust than normal. Would you like to tell me why that wasn't the case?"

Rocco got the distinct feeling that the judge knew everything and was trying to make Matt say it; trying to make him trip over his own story.

"I have an authorised religious exemption from automatic extensions of interest-accruing credit," Matt said, as firmly as he could manage.

The judge nodded slowly. It was the oddest nod Rocco had ever seen; as though she was nodding *no* rather than *yes*.

"It's true," Matt said, the firmness fading. "Look it up! You'll see."

"I wonder, Mr Richmond… does your religion take as dim a view of lying as it does of moneylending?"

Matt gulped loudly enough for Rocco to hear, even over the sound of his own elevated heart-rate.

"We know about your offline assets," the judge said, confirming Matt's worst fear. "We know that you applied for the religious exemption on the same day as all five of your business partners. We know, Mr Richmond. What I *don't* know is why you told the responding officer that you didn't have any money to pay your overdue Travel Duty."

"You can call it a Travel Duty all you want," Steve Keller mumbled, slouched in his chair. "We all know it's a Movement Tax."

"Excuse me?" the judge said.

Steve didn't look up. "You heard."

Rocco kept his own gaze fixed on the wall straight ahead. He respected Steve for saying what he'd just said — for refusing to bend to such an arbitrary exercise of power — but he could ill afford any outward display of agreement and had no inclination to show one; not with his young family just a few steps away, reminding him of what was at stake. Whatever it took to get out of this room and go home, Rocco Miller would do it.

"Listen," Matt said, quite likely saving Steve from the judge's wrath by diverting her attention back to his own case. "I tried to tell the officer I could pay, and I tried to tell the guards. None of them would listen!"

The judge gestured in her left palm, evidently scrolling through the notes relating to Matt's case. "You told one guard on one occasion," she said after a few seconds. "I have footage right here of you telling the responding officer that you couldn't afford to pay your Movement Duty. Now, I'll give you one last chance to explain yourself."

Rocco couldn't even begin to understand Matt's actions. Why would anyone not pay when they had the money? In the seat next to Rocco, Steve Keller was shaking his head and thinking exactly the same thing.

"I was trying to get out of paying the penalty," Matt admitted, his voice breaking under the stress. "I was going to repay the Tax, uh, I mean, the *Duty*. I just wanted to avoid the fine. That's all. I thought that maybe if I said I had no money I could defer—"

"I've heard enough," the judge said, cutting him off. "Let it be recorded that Matt Richmond is hereby sentenced to permanent account termination and indefinite detention for financially motivated crimes against Sycamore."

Matt's mouth opened and closed several times, wordlessly. "In… indefinite?" he eventually echoed.

The judge continued as though he hadn't spoken: "This detention will continue until such a time as a more robust framework of legal provisions is in place to deal with such matters." She looked at the guard behind Matt and nodded.

"No!" Matt protested as the guard yanked him to his feet. "Wait! I have money! I can pay! I have money!"

Matt's brother, a helpless spectator, momentarily rose to his feet and yelled at the escorting guard. The other two guards swiftly removed him from the room via a side exit.

Rocco glanced over to his wife, who looked as worried as he felt.

By the time the guards had returned to their positions behind Rocco and Steve, less than a minute later, Matt Richmond had been taken away through a different door, evidently towards a new and more permanent cell.

The seriousness of Rocco's situation, now apparent, caused a sharp physical pain in his forehead. His sleep-deprived and semi-dehydrated body and mind weren't fit to deal with this kind of stress, and recognising that point only made it even worse.

With everyone bar Steve Keller so evidently reluctant to speak out of turn, the commotion didn't take long to die down.

"I'll go next," Steve said, itching his scraggy beard as the judge looked down at him.

"You were next anyway," she said, keen to maintain her air of control. "So, would you like to tell me why you're here."

"Vagrancy."

"Try again."

"Vagrancy," Steve said.

"No. Travel Duty evasion."

"I don't know what your notes are telling you, but I was arrested for sleeping too close to Sycamore HQ and I was charged with vagrancy."

"That's not the reason you're in my court," the judge said, more disdainful than impatient.

"It's the *only* reason I'm in your court! They put one of these Seeds in my hand because I was charged with a crime, and then they had the gall to tell me I was lucky to get the damn thing for free!"

Rocco still didn't think the room was much of a court, and he was somewhat surprised by the relative eloquence of Steve's words. The vagrancy charge was less surprising, but it didn't strike him as fair that Steve had been punished for having nowhere safe to spend the night.

"And *then*..." Steve went on, "and then they stop me in the street the next day and tell me I'm under arrest for not paying my Movement Tax!? What the hell am I supposed to pay it with? How can they dump me on the street with no money and no credit line then charge me to walk around? And I didn't consent to any terms and conditions like these other guys did, so don't quote any of—"

"Certain rights and privileges are lost when you commit a crime, Mr Keller. But I do agree that your case is not a one-off occurrence. Your problems with the law predate this instance, and in my judgement they appear likely to persist. Given your self-confessed inability to fund your own existence and your general cooperation with law enforcement officers, I see no option but to place you in the care of a local SDU."

Steve's eyebrows rose. "A what?"

"Secure Dependency Unit."

"You're sending me to a madhouse?"

"No," the judge said, pausing to find the right wording, "this is nothing to do with your mental faculties. An SDU is a residential unit for consumers who are temporarily unable to provide for themselves financially but otherwise pose no risk to themselves or society."

"So you're sending me to a *poor*house?"

The judge hesitated again. "Well, I wouldn't use that word."

"Will I have a real bed?" Steve asked, his tone suddenly changing.

"And three meals a day. But let me be clear: your continued presence in the SDU rather than a prison cell is conditional on your continued cooperation with the Unit's compulsory program of activities."

"What kind of activities?"

"Consumer testing, infrequent pharmaceutical testing, things of that nature."

With this mention of compulsory pharmaceutical testing, Steve no longer looked quite so enthused by the prospect. "How long are we talking?"

The judge tipped her head slightly in thought. "Assuming full cooperation — and I do mean *full* cooperation — a man with no significant debts could expect to earn enough to be considered financially capable of returning to society in as little as 30 to 36 months."

Steve quietly digested this timescale. "And how long in prison if I say no?"

"Mr Keller, my firm opinion, both professional and personal, is that your interests would be best served by participation in the SDU program. Given the circumstances of your most recent arrest and your cooperation with the responding officer — on top of your previous history of cooperating with law enforcement — any period of criminal detention would likely be shorter than an SDU stay. But I encourage you to consider the future beyond the next few years. If you see out a custodial sentence and nothing changes, you'll end up straight back in prison as soon as you get out."

After looking at the floor for several thoughtful seconds, Steve met the judge's eyes. "I'll take the SDU," he said.

"I must clarify that there can be no visitation given the nature of the SDU's program of activities."

"I've got no one, anyway," Steve said, motioning his hand towards the seated onlookers. "None of them are with me."

The judge gestured in her palm and asked Steve to wait in his chair until the third case had been heard. "You'll be taken to the SDU within the hour," she said. "Either alone, or with Mr Miller."

~

Rocco sat in awkward silence, opting to wait until he was directly asked to speak. He noticed the buzzing of a white light overhead, which flickered every so often. When the judge finally finished looking through his case notes, she looked at him with disdain.

"Six counts," she said, not even bothering to ask Rocco to explain why he was there. "In order: failure to pay your Travel Duty, resisting arrest, *evading* arrest, failure to comply with a direct system order, trespassing, and a second count of resisting arrest. Have I missed anything?"

Rocco's hands were shaking. Unlike Steve Keller, this was

his first time in any kind of trouble with the law. And unlike Steve Keller, he hadn't come easily when he'd eventually been caught. He shook his head.

"Hmm? Nothing to say for yourself?"

"I acted without thinking," Rocco blurted out. His mind raced at a million miles an hour, having worked through the countless things he wanted to say until it found one that wouldn't make his current situation even worse.

"Six times?"

"It was one incident," Rocco said, trying to keep his voice strong. "It all happened within… I don't know exactly… ten or fifteen minutes."

"Well then, Mr Miller, why don't you quickly tell me what *happened* in those fifteen minutes, to see how your recollection vibes with the reports and the footage in front of me?"

Rocco momentarily glanced at his wife and child then inhaled deeply to gather his composure. "I was fired the night before this all happened," he began, "which is why I couldn't pay. It was nothing like the first guy's case. I don't have any hidden assets and I didn't apply for the religious exemption. I just couldn't get a credit extension because being unemployed and having a new mouth to feed made me too much of a risk. I know the Tax isn't much, but I didn't have *anything*. My balance hit zero when I was going to the hospital to see my son. There he is, right over there."

The judge was visibly irked by Rocco's decision to point towards his young family, apparently in an effort to soften her demeanour. She said nothing, opting to let Rocco continue until he slipped up, as she fully expected he would.

"I had to get to the hospital to see my son, so I went. That's the story. But I didn't force the security guy at the door to let me in. He *chose* to type the code to unlock it, so I don't think it's fair to call that trespassing."

The judge gestured into her palm again, flipping through pages of reports which were visible only in her UltraLenses. "You seem to have left out the part when you resisted and evaded arrest, Mr Miller, not to mention when you resisted *again* after seeing your child at the hospital."

Rocco's eyes narrowed. "Do you know what actually happened? The first responding officer let me go. How can you say I evaded arrest when he stepped back and let me go?"

The judge evaded the question. "And when you were on the way to the hospital," she said, "undertaking a journey you knew fine well you couldn't pay for, did you or did you not throw your UltraLenses from a moving vehicle to avoid the clear and repeated pop-up warnings that what you were doing was illegal and would have serious consequences?"

"Do you know whose car I was in?" Rocco asked.

The judge nodded slightly, her expression uneasy. "But as to my question..."

In that moment, Rocco cottoned on to the fact that the judge didn't want to talk about this issue because she was the only person in the room who knew. "So you *do* know who drove me to the hospital?" he pushed. "You *do* know who told the responding officer to let me go and then asked the doorman at the hospital to let me in? And you *do* know who made it his personal mission to make sure I made that journey and saw my son?"

The judge gulped. "Mr Miller, please stay on topic."

Rocco looked over to his wife once more. "It was Kurt," he said. "Kurt Jacobs."

A collective gasp filled the air.

"The owner of the vehicle is not the issue in question," the judge said.

"Kurt was on my side," Rocco said, fully committing to what he now thought was his only hope of going free. "Kurt *is* on my side. I was fired after messing up his drinks order in the restaurant where I worked, and when he saw me being arrested the next day he felt responsible and stepped in. He was right there, just outside of Sycamore HQ, when he saw me standing with a flashing 'wanted' sign above my head. So you can talk about how I ignored direct orders, but I had a direct order from Kurt Jacobs to get in his car and go to the hospital. If he was here right now, I think we both know what he would say."

"But he's *not* here, Mr Miller."

"So call him! Bring him in; he'll tell you himself.

"Things have changed since you were detained," the judge said. "Mr Jacobs is no longer with us."

"With who? What the hell are you talking about?"

"He's been missing for several days. There was an attack on a vehicle he was supposed to be travelling in. He survived the blast, but he hasn't been seen since. His disappearance is being treated as a kidnapping."

"Jesus," Rocco sighed. He couldn't help but be more concerned about the effect of this news on his own situation than he was about Kurt's wellbeing.

"Now," the judge said, lowering her tone. "Given the circumstances surrounding your eventual detention and your behav—"

"No," Rocco interrupted. "Listen to me: this was all a big misunderstanding. Kurt got me fired and he tried to put it right. I'm not a criminal! I'm a hard worker, you just have to let me prove it. Why send me to prison or an SDU at the public's expense when I can be a productive member of society? I *want* to be a productive member of society. I *will* be. I can go back to waiting tables, or I can work security again like I used to on weekends. All I want is to make a life for my family. I'll do anything. Training, education, military… anything."

The judge leaned back and looked down her nose at Rocco. "*Any*thing?"

"Anything!"

Given Rocco's few weeks of experience in private security, as well as his reasonable level of education and his evident motivation, the judge had an idea. "There's a rehabilitation program," she said, "open to minor offenders who show aptitude for certain roles."

"I'll do it. Whatever it is, I'll do it."

"Enthusiasm is a good thing, Mr Miller, but you have to hear what it is first."

"Okay, okay," Rocco said, smiling at his wife. She smiled back. "Anything."

"There is an urgent need for Travel Duty Enforcement Officers. Your role, should you choose to accept it, will involve making sure that those who attempt to evade their Travel Duty do not succeed in doing so."

"But everything is digital," Rocco said. "It's all debited automatically."

"I'm not talking about debt collection, Mr Miller. I'm talking about enforcement. Some offenders come peacefully, such as Mr Keller here, while others don't. I'm sure you're familiar with the type."

"So I would have to round up people who can't afford to pay their Movement Tax?" Rocco asked. The words stuck in his throat; the Movement Tax was an unjustifiable attack on the poor, and he couldn't bear the thought of facilitating its operation.

"It's a Travel Duty," the judge said flatly. "And yes; in coarse terms, that would be your role. There is, of course, plenty of room at the SDU, should you refuse this offer. Or in prison, should you refuse the SDU."

Rocco looked to his wife once more. Her smile was gone, now replaced by a blank expression.

"You have to do it," Steve Keller said, making no effort to lower his voice. "Taking their deal won't make you any less of a man."

Had that been the sticking point for Rocco, his decision would have been a whole lot easier. Looking at Steve's sullen eyes and malnourished frame, Rocco imagined having to forcibly detain others like him who committed the grievous sin of running out of money. It would be one thing to aid Sycamore in disciplining people like Matt Richmond who had lied in an effort to cheat the system… but people like Steve?

"Your kid needs his dad," Steve went on, reading Rocco's conflicted expression. "Say yes."

Rocco looked up at the judge and gritted his teeth. "Fine."

"I'm sorry?" the judge said, somewhat sarcastically. "I didn't quite hear that."

"He said *fine*," Steve snapped, irked by the judge's unprofessional and uncalled for gloating.

"Very well. Guards, if you would."

At the judge's instruction, one of the guards lifted a small black sheet from her desk — it looked something like a thin slate — and carried it towards Rocco. "Place your left hand on the surface for Seed reactivation," the guard said.

Rocco followed the order.

The other guard then handed Rocco a new pair of Ultra-Lenses, still factory sealed. Rocco opened the box and placed the Lenses against his eyes. He then dismissed the notifications about his newly extended line of credit and the cost of the new Lenses before rising to his feet as instructed.

"You will report for training tomorrow morning," the judge said. "The details will arrive in your inbox shortly. Please see yourself out."

Rocco immediately embraced his wife and son. The tiny baby was asleep, as he had been throughout, and Rocco's wife remained sufficiently silent to suggest she had been warned against speaking.

"Take it outside," the judge said.

Before stepping through the door, Rocco looked back towards Steve Keller, who was looking right back at him with an understanding glint in his eye. "You've gotta do what you've gotta do," Steve said.

"That's enough, Mr Keller," the judge snapped. "Guards, prepare him for transfer to the SDU."

Steve raised a hand to see Rocco off. Rocco could only bring himself to half-nod in reply.

As the external door swung open, the world around Rocco

seemed impossibly bright. There were ads everywhere; even more than there had been five days earlier.

A sudden deluge of incoming messages popped up to fill Rocco's vision as he approached his wife's waiting car, each one congratulating him on the new job.

Correctly assuming that his employment status must have been automatically updated, Rocco looked in the car's wing mirror for a few seconds until his information popped up:

Rocco Miller. 21. Married. Sycamore Agent.

FIVE

Dexter

Dexter awoke to the sound of knocking. The quiet but repetitive clink of knuckles on glass momentarily startled him until he was awake enough to consider the likelihood of who it was. He pulled the cord to open his blinds and sighed with relief at the sight of Kayla's face, as excitable and mischievous-looking as it had been back in the days when these late night visits were far more common.

Kayla, Dexter's childhood best friend and neighbour of more than a decade, then gestured with her hand in an unmistakable request for him to remove his UltraLenses.

"Why?" he mouthed.

Kayla pointed to the bag over her shoulder. Dexter quickly grasped the point that she didn't want him to see whatever was inside while he was wearing his Lenses. He took them out as quickly as he could then opened the window to talk.

"I can't keep taking these out," Dexter said, referencing Kayla's last visit six days earlier. "The system will flag me as suspicious. If there was anything in my life for them to notice, or if I had more Forest friends, it probably would have reprimanded me already. That's what happens. You won't be able to take yours out at all after tomorrow. It'll be different for you."

Kayla didn't pretend to disagree. Though an arbitrary cut-off point had seen the fourteen months she had over Dexter land them two school years apart, she knew he didn't have many friends. When Dexter had first gotten his Seed, right after the launch, he visited Kayla in hospital and tried to cheer her up with a self-deprecating revelation that his Forest account's popularity score fell in the bottom 2% of all school-age children. She could read Dexter better than anyone else could, and she knew that he genuinely didn't mind being anonymous in most people's eyes.

"That's the point," she replied. "Until I figure something out for how to mess with the system, tonight is our last chance to have fun. Get dressed and meet me at the door."

"We have school in three hours!" Dexter protested.

"Not me; I have to go to Tasmart to get my stupid Seed implanted first."

"Fine. *I* have school in three hours."

"I'll have you home in two," Kayla said. "Come on, we're burning moonlight."

"I don't *have* two hours. If I go out and my dad wakes up before I'm home, he'll kill me."

"How many times have I ever gotten you in trouble?" Kayla asked, raising her eyebrows and tilting her head in mock innocence.

Dexter laughed out loud. "You seriously want me to count?"

"Exactly," she said. Her expression flattened. "And how many of those times did I fail to get you out of it?"

Dexter sighed, his original relief at seeing Kayla outside having been long since replaced by a feeling of tired apprehension. "What's in the bag, anyway?"

Kayla smiled in victory and began to descend the ladder.

With ill-tempered streetlights buzzing overhead, Kayla and Dexter set off along their otherwise silent street. The area was run-down, with a declining population and ever-decreasing property values. The nearest point of interest was Barnford Park, an out-of-town industrial park to the north. Local jobs were few and far between and local amenities were disappearing at an alarming rate.

"Where are we going, anyway?" Dexter asked. "And what's in the bag?"

Kayla lifted the bag's strap from her shoulder and handed it to him. "I want to add a design. One of our own. We're going to the old pawnshop with the giant stickman on the wall."

The four cans of spray-paint had already told Dexter what kind of design Kayla was talking about, but her reference to the stickman graffiti gave him pause.

"What's up?" Kayla said, noticing that he'd stopped.

"That one's gone. They cleaned it off sometime between last week and yesterday."

Kayla thought for a few seconds then continued walking. "Fine. All it means is that we have a bigger space to do something cool. Was the thing about Amos still there on the other wall?"

Dexter shook his head.

"So that means we have *two* full walls to work with."

"I guess."

As they neared their destination, Kayla's sudden change of subject caught Dexter by surprise. "So," she said, unusually quietly. "How much does it hurt, anyway?"

"Not much," he said, holding up his left palm to show her the almost invisible Seed-scar.

Kayla then peeled the loose cotton bandage from her own left hand and showed Dexter the still-healing wound, just off-centre. This wound — obtained during an unfortunate and almost fatal altercation with two dogs while she was babysitting for a now-estranged family friend — was the sole reason why Kayla had not yet been forced to take a Seed, as all school-age children now were. Endlessly antipathetic to authority, Kayla had joked to Dexter during his frequent hospital visits that the dogs had done her a favour by buying her two months off school and several weeks without Sycamore's Seed.

Dexter knew there had been serious and prolonged concerns about a vein in Kayla's neck or something like that, but his understanding went no further; Kayla never wanted to talk about it and he never wanted to push her for details. All he knew for sure was that she was lucky to have gotten out of the incident with so little lasting damage and that her left hand looked in no fit state for any kind of implant.

"I asked if they could do it in my right hand," she said, reading the concern on Dexter's face. "But they only do that if you either don't have a left hand or don't have any fingers on your right. The doctor said it should be fine."

Dexter nodded as reassuringly as he could. "They wouldn't say that if it wasn't true. I mean, they're injecting Seeds into *babies* now, so they obviously don't need much room to work with. And it goes in pretty deep, so they can probably do it at an angle and then straighten it once it's in."

"That sounds worse," Kayla said, but the laughter in her voice pierced the glum bubble.

"Your hand will be fine. It's when they inject the Lens-checker into your eyeball… that's when you feel it."

"What? My *eyeball*?"

Dexter's attempt at keeping a straight face to hide his teasing failed almost instantly.

Kayla punched him in the arm. "Asshole."

Before long, they turned the final corner towards the old pawnshop. A familiar message sprayed in large black letters — less than complimentary about Sycamore supremo Isaiah Amos — soon came into view.

"Someone must have sprayed the same thing up again," Dexter said.

"Too bad," Kayla replied. But having originally only wanted to spray a small personal flourish next to the complex stickman design, which had already been encircled by several supportive tags she'd seen from the road as she passed by on her way home from hospital, she was actually somewhat relieved that she wouldn't have to think of something to fill this much larger space.

It was easy to talk big to Dexter about spraying large designs on two walls, but such words were hollow. Kayla was neither much of an artist nor much of a vandal; all she had wanted was to do something exciting with Dexter on her last night without a Seed; on the last night when her every action wouldn't be recorded by a pair of UltraLenses she couldn't remove without arousing suspicion.

Her choice of activity — to spray a small message on the wall of a disused building in a relatively harmless show of support for an exceptional piece of street art — had the added benefit of allowing her to vent some frustration at Sycamore itself, which was the lampooned subject of the graffiti in question. Had she known the graffiti had been cleaned off before Dexter told her, she never would have dreamed of replacing it with her own. But self-imposed peer pressure was a very real thing, so here she was.

"You don't have to do it," Dexter said, reading her thoughts as only he could. "I know you only wanted to add something, not do a whole new one."

Kayla's expression changed completely when she stepped round the corner and looked at the wall where the complex stickman graffiti had been. "I thought you said they cleaned it off?" she said, more confused than anything else.

"They did," Dexter said, hurrying to join her and sounding even more confused. He looked up at the intricate piece of street art — the only apt term — and tried to make sense of it. "I'm telling you: this was gone when I passed by yesterday! Someone must have put it back, just like the Amos thing."

"But everything is the same," Kayla countered. "*Exactly* the same. Look: even the tags and initials in the circle around it are identical. There's Kenny's one… right where it was."

Even without considering the dozens of tags, Kayla knew that the main design was far too complex to have been replicated so perfectly. The central component was a slouched stickman who lay in a barren desert landscape with only cacti and vultures for company. It looked, for want of a better word, *professional*... like a cartoon which just happened to be painted on a wall rather than printed in an old-fashioned magazine. A needle rested in the stickman's right hand while his left dripped with bright red blood which provided the only colour in the otherwise monochrome design. In reference to the runaway success of Happy Pigs, Sycamore's inane farmyard simulator which boasted tens of millions of distraction-seeking players per day, the dying stickman wore a smiling pig mask.

Subtlety wasn't a word anyone would associate with the image, but Kayla felt like that was the whole point.

Dexter mumbled that its presence on the wall didn't make sense as Kayla opened her bag and pulled out a small can of yellow spray-paint. The girl then began to spray on a childlike sunshine, straight-line rays and all. Impressed with her own neatness, she finally reached for the black can to add a "K" to the centre of the still-drying yellow circle.

"Kayla!" Dexter said, getting her attention as quietly as possible.

She turned to see that Dexter had crouched down and was urging her to do the same. He tilted his head towards an alleyway from which he could clearly hear footsteps. Kayla heard them too and crouched down as low as she could.

A woman came into view, with a young-looking spaniel by her side. Rather than holding the dog's leash in her hand, the woman had looped and tied it around her wrist, evidently so that she could freely gesture into her left palm with her right hand's fingers as she walked.

Just when it looked like the passerby would continue without noticing them, her dog let out a string of high-pitched yelps as it noticed the two strangers hiding in the shadows. The dog strained at its leash, most likely in a playful effort to reach the crouching humans, and in doing so almost pulled its inattentive owner off her feet.

"Ruby," the woman snapped, slightly adjusting course to keep her balance. The dog sniffed the air a few inches from Dexter's face until it was pulled away, still yelping, as the woman continued on obliviously.

"How the hell did she not see us?" Kayla asked when she deemed it safe to do so.

"She was fully immersed," Dexter said, familiar with the glazed-over look he'd seen in the woman's eyes. "She was probably using BeThere. It lets you walk around virtual environments while you actually walk around the real world. There's collision detection and—"

"I know what it is. But wouldn't you still show up? You know, since you're seeded?"

"Not if she was using the Unobstructed mode; it hides everyone, not just unseeded people. If the system thought she was about to walk into one of us, it would stop her. But the system hides everything that doesn't fit in with what it wants her to see." Dexter's eyes shot back to the graffiti. "*Wait…*"

Kayla rose to her feet, catching on. "Do you really think?"

"Definitely," Dexter said. "They didn't clean the graffiti at all. They just painted over it in the system! Everyone wearing Lenses sees the world as it is in the universal system settings, not as it actually is. So when I saw this wall yesterday, with my Lenses in, it was blank because that's how it is in the system. That's how it is in *augmented* reality, not actual reality."

"I always thought augmented reality meant adding things. You know, like ads and everything. When did they start hiding stuff? That is like… seriously messed up."

"What I don't get is why they got rid of this graffiti but left every other filthy building exactly as it was. Other towns have had full makeovers with virtual flower beds and water features."

"I bet it's because this is dissent," Kayla said, looking up at the wall with a new and stronger feeling. "This is anti-Sycamore, so they erase it. They don't care about making this place better. They just don't want people to see anything that goes against the company. It's about control. If people think it's okay to badmouth Sycamore, they will. So I bet Sycamore has a roomful of idiots whose entire job is painting over stuff like this, just so no one sees it. What does it say about a system if the people in charge have to hide opposing views because they know those views make sense?"

Dexter didn't say anything for a while. He pretty much agreed with Kayla, but the strength of her views surprised him. "But when you go to get seeded in a few hours, you're going to be stuck *inside* the system."

"It's not like I can say no," Kayla said, somewhat defensively. "But it's also not like I have to mean it when I say yes."

"Huh?"

"Just because I have to play their game, that doesn't mean I have to want them to win. Taking the Seed just means they think I'm on their side. And *that* means I have them right where I want them. That means their guard is down."

"For what?"

"Do you want to do one before we leave?" Kayla asked, inelegantly changing the subject and handing Dexter her bag to indicate what she meant. "Because we should probably get going."

"What's the point of me spraying something if no one is going to see it? It's like that thing about a tree falling in the woods."

"*I'll* see it," Kayla said. "And *they'll* see it."

Dexter hesitated.

"This is your chance to stick a middle finger up to Sycamore without getting in trouble. Like you said, you can't keep taking your Lenses out. When will you have another chance to show them how you feel about them replacing reality with their candy-coated corporate garbage?"

Dexter opened the bag and pulled out the blue can and the smaller of the two alphabet stencils. He had some experience at this, but, ironically enough, he and Kayla had previously always looked for the most isolated canvasses they could find so that their pointless teenage messages *wouldn't* be seen by anyone else. "Don't look yet," he said.

Kayla turned away until Dexter announced that he was finished, at which point she looked. She saw Dexter's message written beside her own yellow sunshine, short and to the point. The message contained one word on each of two lines, horizontally centred: "SYCAMORE SUCKS!"

"Concise," she said, laughing softly.

Dexter shrugged. "The truth always is."

SIX

Stavros

With essay deadlines and exam dates looming, Stavros 'Stav' Georgiou sat quietly with his friend Max Jasper in the usual booth of their local pub. As the least studenty drinking establishment either of them knew, this pub, located directly beneath their shared flat on the outskirts of London, was the perfect place to forget about the responsibilities of university.

Both were good students in that they caused no problems and handed their work in on time, but neither had ever applied themselves fully. They already shared deep regret over all the time they had wasted doing nothing, particularly since the nature of their university's grading system — which gave equal weight to all modules taken in a student's final two years — meant that previous mediocre performances had already locked them into lower final marks than they had hoped for. That the grades awarded for their ongoing modules would have no effect on their degree classifications was more depressing than it was liberating.

While Stav tried to shake all course-related thoughts out of his mind to enjoy the evening as best he could, he noticed Max fiddling with a phone on the other side of the booth. This in itself was unusual for Max, who wasn't the most social of creatures, but Stav was primarily intrigued by *which* phone Max was holding.

"Why have you got that thing with you?" Stav asked, looking across at a well-used Systelonik XK6 he hadn't seen for more than a year. "Did your new phone break?

Max grinned and performed a few quick gestures on the phone's touchscreen before holding it out at arms length so Stav could see.

Stav looked at the screen and saw his own face moving in real time. "You must have accidentally done the gesture to launch the front-facing camera," he said.

"Nope."

"Look," Stav insisted, holding the phone up to show him. "It's showing me."

Max grinned. "Keep watching."

Stav returned his gaze to the screen, which still showed his face. Max turned his head to the wall while still holding the phone in front of Stav. Immediately, Stav gasped in amazement — his face left the screen and was replaced by the peeling wallpaper Max was staring at.

Max turned back to Stav, grinning even more.

Stav sat stunned; not by what he'd just seen, but by what he knew it meant. He leaned in excitedly and whispered: "You've got... Lenses? Linked to an XK6?"

Max nodded proudly and lowered the phone. "100% legit Sycamore UltraLenses," he said. "Fully hacked and linked to this phone, which is loaded with homebrew apps built specifically for the Lenses."

"Like what?"

"Lie detector, facial recognition, real-time zoom... everything you get with the AR glasses you can buy here, plus more. But the best thing is: no one knows I'm using them. This has always been the best phone in the world for homebrew, and the scene has been kick-started again by the Lens-hack. There are so many possibilities."

Stav leaned back against his cushioned seat, deep in

thought over how they could best leverage this huge social advantage. His first thought was that it would enable them to cheat on their exams, which would have been useful a few months ago when their grades still made a difference.

"You want a game, Stav?" a loud voice interrupted. It belonged to Chuck, one of the pub's dozen or so middle-aged regulars who all liked the boys and welcomed the respectful hint of youth they brought to the pub. Chuck stood by the pool table, holding a cue in his hand.

Stav had never beaten Chuck in almost forty attempts, but he always enjoyed the chat. "Just a sec," he called back.

"Play for a pint?" Chuck asked.

"That'll be right!" Stav laughed, rising to his feet. "I might as well just give you my bank card."

As Chuck racked up the balls, Max noticed a glint in Stav's eye. "What are you thinking?" he asked, smiling to mirror Stav's excited expression.

Stav leaned in close and whispered: "We're going to build an app that helps us cheat at pool."

~

"All we need are lines telling us which way the balls will go after we hit them," Stav said, still grinning about his idea after another three convincing defeats to Chuck. He stood over Max in their flat above the pub, reading the computer screen as Max searched for information about existing ball physics apps for AR glasses.

The most responsive and reliable systems used ceiling mounted cameras to communicate with the user's glasses, since a bird's-eye view was naturally superior to looking at balls from eye-level when it came to predicting their post-impact movements. Max found an old open source app intended for snooker coaching which used perspective to annotate the table with the distances and angles between the object and target ball, as well as between the target ball and target pocket. Max would be able to use the guts of this code for his own app. Unfortunately, however, there were going to be limitations.

"There's no way I can make this work in real time," Max said. He had plenty of experience in app development, but most of it had been several years ago and none of it had dealt with so many live variables. "The best I can realistically do — and this is a big *maybe* — is to overlay an optimal shot-line. It won't be like the system in the 8-ball video we watched a few minutes ago; the lines won't move when you change the angle of the cue or anything like that."

"A shot-line is all we need," Stav said. "How will it work?"

Max knew that Stav didn't really want to know how it would *work*, but rather how it would *look* and what he would have to do. "You'll look at the shot from the natural angle," he said, "and I'll take a snapshot on the phone and feed that into the app. I'll use the virtual table to find the exact potting angle, then overlay the shot-line onto the real table. All you have to do then is line your cue up along the line and hit the ball straight. It'll look like one of the pool games you get for normal phones, except it's real."

"How are you going to overlay the line onto the table, though?"

Again, Max was wary that Stav wouldn't understand too many specifics. "There's this app — *Decorate XL* — made by another English guy called Burf. It lets you overlay anything anywhere. That handles the overlay. But the hardest part will be calibrating *my* app to the dimensions of the real table. You'll have to look straight into each corner pocket from all four sides of the table before we start. It's on you to find a way to do that without looking suspicious. Then I'll put a grid on the table — and it's on you to not smile like an idiot or react to that in any way — and after that it's just a case of you lining up the shot as best you can and me using the app to line up the actual potting angle. Do you get it?"

Stav nodded. "Will it show where the cue ball will go after contact, too? Assuming I don't put any spin on it?"

"Hopefully," Max said.

Understanding that time was against them, Max didn't leave his desk for the next eight hours. Sycamore's UltraLenses had never officially been sold in the UK; until the US launch of The Seed a few weeks earlier, UK consumer awareness of Sycamore's products had been almost zero. That was changing rapidly and would continue to do so. As such, Max knew that any competitive advantage they could derive from his hacked UltraLenses and custom apps would last only as long as the public's obliviousness to the fact that the Lenses had been hacked to allow unauthorised third-party apps and that a handful of British tech enthusiasts were discreetly using them with the aid of two-year-old smartphones.

While Max worked, delighted by the adaptability of the snooker-coaching app, Stav headed out to a 24-hour supermarket and returned with a small foldable pool table, just four feet in length.

11 hours of sleep and 37 hours of focused work later, Max woke Stav in the middle of the night to tell him it was time to test out the new app he had unoriginally title "Pool Hack".

Max handed Stav his hacked UltraLenses after placing them in the provided cleaning pod. Stav excitedly put the Lenses in his eyes for the first time and followed Max's instructions to stand at one end of the small table, which was set up with two balls: the cue ball and the black.

"Look at each corner pocket for half a second," Max said. Stav did so. "Move to the other end and do the same. Be subtle." Stav managed the first part but struggled with the subtlty. Max wasn't concerned; if Stav's easy-to-correct awkwardness was the biggest problem they ran into, they'd be laughing.

"Now do I go back round and look at the shot?" Stav asked.

"Wait." Max gestured on his phone's screen and, thanks to the code base he borrowed from the Decorate XL app, tapped a button to overlay a static grid onto Stav's real-time view of the table.

Stav's stunned expression immediately told Max that it had worked.

"*Now* look at the shot," Max said. "Blink twice when you think you've lined it up."

Just six or seven seconds later, Stav's expression turned from stunned to awe-struck as a series of laser-like blue lines appeared on the table to guide his shot. He took care to line his cue up perfectly then played the shot. To his delight, the black ball fell nicely into the centre of the tiny target pocket. But even better, the cue ball also precisely followed its predicted post-contact line of travel.

"We're going to be rich," he said, beaming at Max.

"Calm down," Max said. "People who are really good at pool already see these lines in their heads. We need to be careful who we play and be careful not to get carried away. A few big wins here and there is all we need, so we should use the lie detector and face-reader apps to tell who's drunk, who's bluffing, and who's trying to hustle us. We'll pick when to strike, and then we'll strike. Hard."

"I want to practice against Chuck," Stav said. "When I can beat him, we'll look for bigger games."

"You'll practice against yourself," Max insisted, his tone leaving no room for argument. "When I say you're ready, you can try it against Chuck. But it has to be seamless; your subtlety is what we need to work on as much as anything else."

"How about we practice all day then play Chuck tonight? I want to beat him."

"You'll play when I say you're ready," Max said flatly.

Stav nodded in acceptance. "Let's get to work."

~

"Fancy a game, Stav?" Chuck asked after dispatching his latest challenger.

"Why not," Stav replied. "I've been practising. I worked out what I was doing wrong."

"Oh yeah?"

Stav nodded, as rehearsed. "I hadn't been closing one of my eyes to line up the shot. Me and Max have been playing on a tiny table upstairs and now that I've worked it out, I literally can't miss. I've always known what shot to play, but now I can actually play it."

Chuck laughed heartily. "Put a pint on it?"

"Call it twenty quid," Stav said.

This got the attention of the other drinkers.

"Your funeral," Chuck said, racking up the balls.

Stav turned to Max, who was still seated, and winked. He then stood at each end of the table and looked at the corner pockets with as much subtlety as possible, distracting Chuck with talk about how much bigger this table was than the one he'd been practising on.

"We don't really have to play for twenty quid," Chuck said, kindly offering Stav a way out.

A perfect grid appeared on the table before Stav's eyes. He strove to contain his delight. "A deal's a deal," he shrugged.

Four minutes later, Stav was £20 richer.

"Double or quits," Chuck suggested.

Stav exaggerated another shrug. "Your funeral."

All of the pub's regulars crowded around the table to watch. After a slightly more protracted battle, Stav came out on top once again. His previous games against Chuck and the other regulars had given him a good grounding in the basics of ball control, and now that an idiot-proof series of blue lines guided his every shot, he was too much for Chuck to handle.

"Double or quits," Chuck suggested again.

Instantly, Max disabled the app.

Stav saw the grid vanish from the table and understood that Max wanted him to stop. He counted the crowd — nine including himself, Max and Chuck — and shook his head. “Forty’s enough. Pints all round,” he said to the barman, pointing to Chuck to indicate that he would be paying.

The other regulars cheered and patted Stav on the back. A written message appeared in his vision, typed by Max: “Offer to play the others for free. Deliberately miss every shot I don’t overlay. I’ll reset the grid before each game so you can practice calibrating the table without looking suspicious.”

Stav spent the rest of the night winning some and losing some, each game’s outcome dependent on the importance of the shots Max ordered him to miss. As the night wore on and the crowd slowly dwindled, Chuck took a seat across from the ever-quiet Max.

“He’s good,” Chuck said. “Apart from some of those shots when he seems to take his eye off the ball, he’s *good*.”

“Good enough to make money?” Max asked, wasting no time.

Chuck nodded and slid Max a scrap of paper containing an address. “My nephew used to play there before he moved away. Good tournaments, good one-on-ones. Stav will be able to play for as much as he wants; there’s always someone willing. But the higher you go, you know… the realer it gets. It’s not a rough place, but there can be some guys you don’t want to mess with.”

“Why are you giving this to *me*?” Max asked.

“You’re the smart one. If he goes, you need to go with him to keep him out of trouble.”

Max considered the words. “How much could we make in a night without risking… anything?”

“Not too much in one night, and especially not too much from one guy. If you win a few one-on-ones then win the monthly tournament, one big night could easily clear three grand without raising too many eyebrows. But don’t let him enter the tournament the first night he goes; that makes him look too confident… like he’s hustling. Let him find his feet, win some games, get some rep. If people don’t know he’s good and he waltzes in and takes all their money, that doesn't end well. But if he proves he's good and they still challenge him, he can win big without finding trouble. You follow?"

Max nodded, even though it all sounded more complicated than he'd expected. Chuck looked and sounded like the kind of guy who knew what he was talking about. Max paid close attention to his advice and would relay it all to Stav.

"Won't it seem weird if I don't play?" Max wondered out loud.

"So play! Knock a few balls around. There are always plenty of guys playing for fun or practising by themselves. It's not some underground elite pool hall, it's just the closest place where guys go to play for decent stakes."

Chuck stood up and left, knocking twice on the table as he always did.

"What was all that about?" Stav asked when he rejoined Max having noticed his long conversation with Chuck.

Max slid the piece of paper across the table. "Our way in."

~

The following evening, after another long day of practice interrupted only by attendance at two frustratingly compulsory morning lectures, Max and Stav took two buses to the pool hall recommended by Chuck. They stood outside, wondering what the other side of the door would look like.

While Max hesitated and prepared to voice his second thoughts, Stav walked in and left him no choice but to follow.

Max immediately relaxed at the sight of smiling faces and the general feeling of the light atmosphere. Like Chuck had said, it was just a pool hall. Max saw a sign-up sheet on the wall for the monthly tournament, with room for 32 entrants each paying a £50 buy-in. £150 would go to each beaten semi-finalists, £300 to the beaten finalist, and £1000 to the winner. With eight days left there were plenty of empty slots remaining, so Max guided Stav away from the sign-up sheet for now.

On a vacant table in the corner of the hall, Stav practiced his new technique for calibrating the table in a subtle manner. He stood a slight distance from the bottom cushion while the balls were racked up — on this occasion by Max, who still had to tap a button on the phone each time Stav's vision centred on one of the corner pockets — then finalised the calibration by looking at the same pockets from the baulk cushion just before playing his first shot. The grid appeared right on cue.

Max quickly realised that he couldn't play while also controlling the app via his phone. He ordered a drink and sat down with it while Stav played solo. After a while, as the surrounding tables began to fill up, a young man around their age challenged Stav to a friendly game.

Max sent a message to the Lenses, telling Stav to play for free and to play as well as he could.

Stav won convincingly, three games in a row.

"You're good," his beaten opponent readily admitted.

With £300 cash in his pocket — an amount he and Max had jointly decided upon — Stav was keen to start playing for real. "Thanks," he said. "Do you think I should enter the tournament?"

"You should play my brother. He got beat in the final last time, so if you can give *him* a good game, you should go for it."

"Is he here?"

"He's on his way. He only plays cash games, though. You good for £100?"

Max typed the word "Yes" so that it appeared in Stav's vision. Win or lose, accepting a challenge at the opponent's requested price was a strong way to build legitimacy among the hall's clientele.

"Definitely," Stav said. "Anything up to £300."

Stav's beaten opponent widened his eyes in surprise. "Probably just the ton," he said. "We'll see what he says. It should only be ten minutes or something; he's on his way."

When the man left Stav alone at the table, Max walked over. "What the hell was that? We said to match any bet under £300, not to raise any bet *up* to £300! Now the guy will probably back out because he knows you're so confident."

"Nah, he'll play."

Fifteen minutes later, doubts began to creep in.

After another five minutes, Stav's previous opponent reappeared and announced that his brother couldn't make it. "He got called in to work," the man said. "How about tomorrow?"

Max seriously doubted that the game would ever take place and struggled to hide his anger at Stav for blowing it by opening his greedy mouth.

"Cool," Stav said. "Tomorrow it is." Tired from a long day's practice, he then suggested to Max that they call it a night. Max agreed.

"You're such an idiot," Max moaned as they left the hall.

Stav didn't say anything. Even though the initial idea to make a pool app had been his idea, Max was the one who put it all together. The UltraLenses and the phone which made it all possible also belonged to Max, which meant that his word was the law.

"How did you feel, anyway?" Max asked as they reached their bus stop at a dark and quiet street corner. "Did you ever feel like you were going to miss?"

Stav smiled. "Never. As long as I keep it simple and don't rely on any bounces off the cushions, the lines—"

Before Stav could complete his thought, an unseen figure aggressively shoved him into the bus stop's advertising panel. As Max tried to rush forward, another man grabbed him and held his arms behind his back.

"£300," barked the man holding Stav. "Hand it over."

Struggling to free himself, Max saw enough of the man restraining him to know that it was Stav's beaten opponent from twenty minutes earlier; the opponent who, thanks to Stav's big mouth, knew exactly how much money he had. The man holding Stav looked enough like the opponent for Max to assume it was his older, and much larger, brother.

Stav's protests and attempts at resistance were met with

steadily increasing force. After watching one solid blow to the face, Max had seen enough and begged him to hand over the money. Stav relented.

"And your phone," the older brother said.

Max considered rushing forward into the large man, hoping that doing so would break the grip of his own restrainer. He thought better of this idea upon reflecting that he and Stav would have been just as out of their depths in a footrace as they were in a confrontation.

"Just give him it," Max said.

Stav begrudgingly handed over his phone, wishing every second that a bus or at least a passing pedestrian would show up to frighten the muggers away.

With Stav's phone in his hand, the man turned to Max. "And yours. Come on… phone! Now."

Max saw no way out other than handing it over.

"Couple of mugs," the younger of the two brothers said as they walked off. Max heard them laughing and joking about his "stone-age phone" as their voices faded into the distance. Suddenly, the younger brother stopped walking and handed Max's Systelonik XK6 to his brother.

"We have to run," Max said urgently.

Stav, nursing a worsening black eye, looked up from the ground to see that Max was already on his way. "What's going on?"

"Run!"

With a good head start, they were able to evade the brothers until they reached a junction which enabled them to escape unseen.

"Why did you start running?" Stav asked as they began to slow down.

"The app is open on my phone," Max said. "It's called *Pool Hack*. They know we were going to hustle them."

"Ah."

"Thanks to your stupid mouth! If you hadn't said you would play for anything up to—"

"What's done is done," Stav interrupted. "And at least they didn't get your Lenses. Can you buy another one of those phones and fix it so you can add custom apps again?"

"We're never doing this again," Max said, guessing where Stav's thoughts were headed.

"I know that, but hear me out."

"What is there to hear?"

"My idea."

"*What* idea?" Max groaned impatiently.

"Poker."

Already at walking pace since reaching safety, Max stopped moving altogether and considered the idea.

It certainly made more sense than pool, which was much harder to cheat at and had only ever come up as a possibility because Chuck had happened to challenge Stav to a game at the precise moment when Max was telling him about the hacked Lenses.

"We only need two things to have a huge advantage," Stav said. "Being able to read people's faces and instantly spot their tells is the first thing, and knowing the exact percentage chance of winning a hand is the other. There must already be an app for *some* pair of AR glasses which can recognise cards and run the probabilities. Between that and the face-reader thing you already have, all you'd need to do is combine them into one app. Then I would play while you control the phone from however far away the wireless link still works. What do you think?"

The more Max thought about it, the more sense it made. Poker players looked carefully at each other's faces anyway, so there would be no need for subtlety on Stav's part.

"And there are live poker games at *way* more places than cash games of pool," Stav continued before Max could reply. "We can practice every single night at the casino with low stakes, ironing out the kinks and getting used to everything, and we won't look out of place. Casinos sometimes make you put your hand in a scanner to check for The Seed now, in case there are any Americans trying to cheat, and I think they ban phones from live tables, but you'll have the phone at the bar or whatever. It's perfect! Don't you think?"

"You put in all the starting money and we split all winnings 50/50," Max said, driving a hard bargain which he hoped would keep Stav from being reckless. "I already have to buy another XK6 because of your mouth, so that's the deal."

Stav, black eye and all, stood smiling in the darkness. He held out his hand; Max shook it.

"Max, my man…" he said, looking up at the night's slowly clearing clouds. "We're going to be rich."

SEVEN

Damian

Damian Dangerman, former video game streamer and now the second most-watched SycaStar in all of Star's Eye View, sat alone in his lounge as he recovered from a particularly hard day's work.

"Alone" was something of a misnomer, of course, given that Damian's participation in Star's Eye View opened up every moment of his life to whoever felt like watching it through a fully immersive first-person view. The current number of simultaneous viewers, a figure always visible in the lower right corner of Damian's vista, sat at an all-time high of 2.6 million.

Billed as the world's first 24-hour stuntman, Damian's popularity came from his willingness to do things no one else would. His stunts were usually more painful than dangerous, with today's main event having been even more painful than usual. The toes on Damian's left foot were badly crushed and likely broken by the stunt, which lasted no more than a few seconds and involved a bodybuilder dropping an iron dumbbell onto Damian's exposed foot from waist height. Despite local anaesthesia and post-stunt painkilling injections, the pain had continued to find a way through until a delivery of super-strength pills arrived in the early evening.

Some behind-the-scenes staff in the Star's Eye View department at Sycamore HQ had voiced their concerns over potential interactions between the painkillers and Damian's social anxiety medication, but the show had to go on.

Now, in the 9pm primetime hour, Damian couldn't feel anything.

Damian's non-stunt downtime consisted largely of the things he would have been doing anyway, like watching action movies and playing video games. To make these mundane activities appealing to the viewing masses, Star's Eye View directors had recently recruited a stable of comedians and other entertainment personalities to chat with Damian. The resulting discussions resembled something between old DVD commentaries and comedy podcasts. Combined with the "anything can happen" nature of Damian's stream and the hubbub of activity in his lightly moderated chatbox, the smart-mouthed commentators made this Star's Eye View channel the go-to place for an otherwise underserved demographic: bored teenage boys.

Damian didn't mind taking the untested anxiety pills, which smashed through his social discomfort and freed his tongue to hold its own against the incessant ribbing he received from his nightly roundtable of audio jokers. If anything, Damian actually enjoyed the frequent barrages of pull-no-punches jokes at his expense; his guest stars, paid or not, felt like the cool friends he'd never had.

The current game being projected on the virtual screen locked to Damian's wall was SycaCity, a soon to be released city-building game. The "free" game would aggressively push an array of wallet-busting in-app purchases to its players, but Damian didn't have to worry about such things. A discreet message popped up in Damian's vision every now and then, reminding him to drink some Lexington GamerJuice and emphasise how much it was helping his concentration.

Above and below the main screen, each viewer saw animated advertisements precisely targeted to their interests and consumer history. Since the core goal of Star's Eye View was to keep viewers watching for as long as possible, none of these ads were directly clickable. If the ad placements worked — which they usually did — consumers would subconsciously internalise the messages and make the relevant purchasing decisions at a later time.

"I'm getting hungry," Damian said upon completing a new building in his SycaCity, breaking a concentrated silence which had been filled by his guest stars' endless chatter. "Vote *pizza* or *Chinese*."

Damian looked over to his chatbox's word cloud after a minute or so. The word Chinese was far more prominent than pizza — indicating a clear winner — but a different word appeared larger still: Trixi.

It was unprecedented for a post-vote word cloud to be dominated by anything other than one of the binary options so Damian knew that something big was going on with Trixilicious, the only SycaStar with more viewers than him.

Damian knew better than to mention another SycaStar, particularly Trixi, so he slyly performed a gesture in his left palm to pull up a private chat box with his Sycamore rep. This was the only type of vista overlay which could be seen by Damian but not his viewers, who normally saw whatever menu screen he pulled up. Damian quickly typed a question about what was happening on Trixi's stream. Unusually, there was no immediate reply.

After several seconds and several prompts from his guest stars, Damian returned his focus to the result of his latest vote and promptly placed his food order.

The words "Curtis is typing a reply" soon appeared in Damian's private chat overlay, capturing his attention. Damian's guest stars kept talking about SycaCity and their favourite Chinese food as though Trixilicious wasn't utterly dominating the word cloud.

But between the sudden explosion of Trixi-based discussion and the unusual delay in hearing back from Curtis, SycaCity and chicken chow mein were the last things on Damian's mind.

Curtis Dillon had re-entered Damian's life just a few short week's prior to the launch of Sycamore's revolutionary Seed. In those days Damian had scraped a living as a video game streamer, supplementing his income from private walk-throughs by offering a custom design service in which he created uncannily accurate in-game characters. When a request came in one day from a user calling himself Curtis_Crush_Kill, Damian immediately recognised the attached image.

Damian refused the job, claiming he was too busy while keeping the true reason to himself.

Curtis saw through it. "Come on, man," he pleaded. "It's not like your hair didn't grow back."

After a few minutes of back and forth, during which Curtis half-heartedly apologised for giving Damian such a hard time in school, he offered a price that was too good to refuse. Begrudgingly, Damian got to work.

Curtis, just a few years older than Damian at 32, was thoroughly impressed. "Nice job!" he beamed. "That's all the work I need right now, but I'll put something big in your tip jar if you do one more thing…"

"What?"

"Flamin' Damian," Curtis said.

Before Damian had a chance to tell Curtis there was no way he was going to set his hair on fire, as Curtis and his gang cruelly had more than 15 years earlier, a conditional tip appeared in Damian's online tip jar. There were not one but two extra zeroes beyond the kind of offer Damian had expected. He knew Curtis had retired ridiculously young after a profitable decade as a bond trader, but he hadn't realised until now just how profitable that decade must have been.

Damian didn't ask why Curtis wanted this so much; the

conditional tip — worth almost as much as Damian had earned in the last year — had a 10-minute time limit, and Damian quite literally could not afford to let it slip. With neither pride nor shame, he began to negotiate the rules. It was agreed that Damian could apply a barrier of petroleum jelly on his forehead, ears and neck to prevent skin burns in the eight seconds that the flames had to go untouched.

Curtis got what he wanted.

Despite falling off his chair during the act, Damian suffered no serious burns. He also experienced significantly less hair damage than when Curtis and his friends had caught him off guard with an aerosol can and a box of matches all those years ago.

Damian went to bed that night with a smile on his face, in a more comfortable financial position than ever before and with no clue that his "private" performance was already going viral.

If the following morning was crazy, the following weeks were unbelievable. Pushed into it by Curtis, Damian rebranded his streaming channel "Flamin' Damian" and cashed in on his viral fame by performing a variety of so-called stunts which were made available only to paying viewers. In the third week, Curtis informed Damian that he had managed to secure an interview with Sycamore staff who had an interesting offer to make. This offer, for a place on the roster of Sycamore's upcoming Star's Eye View platform, was worth so much money that Damian didn't even have to think about it.

The Star's Eye View staff saw Damian as the perfect online personality to round out their offerings, most of which were heavily geared towards a female viewership. Curtis shoehorned himself into the picture by offering his services to Sycamore, insisting that he would be happy to perform the duties of Damian's rep, free of charge. Given how much profitable attention Curtis had already brought to Damian, everyone agreed that this was a good idea. The revenue sharing agreement between Damian and Curtis, which saw

Curtis net 30% of all Damian's income, had nothing to do with Sycamore.

The hardest Curtis ever worked was in the few days before Star's Eye View went live, during which he had to convince several psychologists and other health professionals that Damian's mental faculties were not sufficiently stunted to render him incapable of making informed decisions about his life-transforming participation in the program and his legal change of name to Damian Dangerman. By hook or by crook, Curtis succeeded.

Not even Curtis could have foreseen the level of popularity Damian's Star's Eye View channel quickly attained. While it was certainly true that Damian's core viewership didn't fall within a traditionally hot demographic for advertising — and while endorsements from Damian weren't in the same universe of profitability as endorsements from someone like Trixilicious, whose Midas touch could turn any given cosmetic or lifestyle product into an instant bestseller — the rapt attention of school-age boys was an elusive and thus valuable commodity.

SycaStars like Trixilicious generated serious revenue through their VIP chatboxes, which were open only to those who paid an extortionate hourly rate for the privilege of having at least one of their comments personally addressed by their chosen SycaStar. Damian didn't have the same kind of fans; neither the creepy older men nor the obsessed teenage girls who went wild upon hearing their idol say their name. Instead, Damian's revenue was generated directly through the stunts he performed.

All Star's Eye View channels were free to watch, no matter how hard Curtis lobbied for an exemption. Curtis got around these rules by offering a public poll to decide each stunt that Damian would next perform, with viewers asked to vote with their wallets. Though he could place no restrictions on the live stream, Curtis created an on-demand library of Damian's past stunts in which each replay was accessible only to those who had voted in the relevant poll. The cost of a vote was almost zero, but the scale of Damian's viewership ensured that it soon added up.

To further encourage votes, Curtis made a habit of including only two options in each stunt poll: one exciting, and one not. This created a sense of urgency even among viewers who had no interest in accessing the on-demand library; if they wanted to see a decent stunt even once, they would have to vote for it to make sure it won.

On the rare occasions when Damian had second thoughts about one of the stunts he was asked to perform, he talked it over with Curtis during a portion of his 20 minutes of daily bathroom privacy. On one solitary occasion, Damian's complaint was more general: he didn't like what he was doing. Curtis told him he was continuing a long tradition dating back to the travelling freak shows of old, which hardly made Damian feel any better. Curtis had no answer to Damian's comment that a large chunk of his viewers were worse than the leering crowds of the freak show era given that they weren't merely tuning in to laugh at Damian, but were in many cases watching in the hope that he would get seriously hurt.

Following a most unexpected turn of events, Curtis Dillon now paced frantically in his uptown penthouse, wracking his brains for a way to stop these misery-seeking viewers from fleeing en masse in Trixi's direction.

~

"Someone just told me that Trixi's whole stream is down," one of Damian's guest star's said, breaking protocol by mentioning a rival SycaStar. "She's never been gone for so long. Nowhere near it."

Reluctant to draw any further attention to Trixilicious, Damian didn't reply. After ten seconds or so he realised that *no one* had replied, and he could only assume that his guest stars had been muted until they sufficiently understood that other

SycaStars were not an acceptable topic of conversation, no matter how unique the situation.

In the silence, Damian's eyes drifted back to his chatbox's word cloud. As he looked, the words *Trixi* and *Trixilicious* — previously the two largest by far — vanished completely. *Chinese* was now the dominant word, reflecting the recent binary vote over his next meal. Damian also noticed an obvious slowdown in messages being posted in the public chatbox, which he correctly assumed to reflect a temporary auto-filter of all comments which mentioned or indirectly referenced Trixilicious.

Damian then looked to the lower right corner of his vista to see if the problems with Trixi's stream were causing viewers to switch over to his, which was the next most popular. To his surprise and dismay, his simultaneous viewership count was falling.

Had it been within the realm of possibility, Damian would have tuned in to Trixi's stream to see for himself what was going on. And had he been able to do so, he would have seen why he wasn't gaining viewers.

The stated purpose of Star's Eye View was to allow viewers to truly feel as though they were living someone else's life. Some streamers' audiences, like Damian's, didn't really want to live vicariously through their favourite SycaStar. But other audiences, primarily Trixi's, almost universally did. Trixi's life was the 24-hour live action version of a lifestyle previously only seen in carefully planned and perfectly lit "spontaneous" photographs of wardrobes full of designer clothes, plates full of artfully presented food, and quiet nights in and big nights out with the girls. The more hours a viewer logged with any given SycaStar, the more attached to the lifestyle they became. For this reason, the screen shown during any downtime didn't encourage viewers to switch over to another SycaStar but rather displayed recent highlights of their favourite SycaStar's stream and promised that normal service would resume imminently.

While Trixi's offline stream did nothing to direct her viewers to Damian or any other SycaStar, speculation about the reasons for her downtime had spread like wildfire in Damian's chatbox from the second it was first mentioned. Had Damian fully understood the internal workings of Star's Eye View, he would have understood why his viewership count was dropping like a stone.

The next few seconds provided an assault on Damian's senses as his guest stars' voices returned to his ears and an urgent message from Curtis appeared in his vista.

Damian tried to focus solely on the message. It explained that Trixilicious was "pretty much having a breakdown" and was dangerously close to exceeding her daily allowance of private bathroom time, but no one knew whether going over the limit by a few minutes would really lead to any punishment for Trixi given how much revenue she generated and how keen everyone at Sycamore was to keep her sweet. Curtis said that Star's Eye View staff first thought she might have been holding the service to ransom and demanding a pay increase, but that they now realised no actress in the world could fake the kind of hysteria she was exhibiting.

"She says she just can't do it any more," Curtis said. "They're even talking about sending someone to help her — in person — to talk her round and make sure she doesn't do anything stupid. But the whole thing is drama. Her fans are watching and waiting because they're so worried about her, and casual viewers are tuning in to see what she does. Everyone loves a car crash."

"Do you think she'll be alright?" Damian typed in reply.

Curtis responded immediately: "Who cares? This is our chance."

Partly out of his desperation to stop haemorrhaging viewers and partly to position Damian as the most talked about SycaStar left standing should Trixi's stream never return, Curtis then informed Damian of his decision to bring the next day's big stunt forward to tonight.

Damian managed to refrain from voicing his anger, which was more than Curtis had expected, and instead responded via their private text window to make clear that he would be doing no more stunts until the morning. The pain in his foot was forcing its way through the painkillers again now that he was thinking about it, and something about the calculated attempt to cash-in on Trixi's troubles didn't sit well with him.

Just as Damian tapped to send his reply to Curtis, one of his guest stars spoke up to reveal that the wheels were already in motion.

"Why don't you do another stunt before your food arrives?" the comedian said, pretending he wasn't reading from a script that Curtis was constantly updating.

"My foot is too sore," Damian said. But he saw the word *stunt* light up the chatbox's word cloud even as he spoke, and he knew it was too late. Once the collective viewership decided that they wanted something, he quite simply had to deliver.

A new message from Curtis popped up: "You'll get three days off next week and a bonus payment tonight."

"How much?" Damian replied.

A number appeared in Damian's vista, precisely ten times larger than the tip Curtis had given him for performing the Flamin' Damian stunt that had set all of this in motion. It was a ridiculous number which quickly quelled Damian's hesitation.

"Okay," he wrote.

Another of Damian's guest stars then jumped in with some stunt suggestions, pretending, like his colleague, that Curtis wasn't behind every word. "Okay," the man said. "How about a flash poll: three minutes, two choices, one stunt. Option 1 is going to be… hmm… you have to cover your face in peanut butter and sit outside until five different dogs lick your face."

Damian instantly got a sinking feeling in his stomach; not because the peanut butter stunt sounded bad, but rather because it *didn't*. Curtis included degrading but mundane options like that when he wanted the other option to win. And given how desperate Curtis was to arrest and reverse the sudden viewer exodus, Damian didn't even want to think about what kind of stunt he had in mind.

The other guest stars voiced their disapproval of this boring option, as if it was necessary to push the voters towards whatever option was coming next.

"Or... you have to dress up in a deer costume and stand in the middle of the highway until someone or something moves you off the road. You can't move of your own will. You can't move at all. You can only *be* moved. Or carried."

"By who?" Damian asked, not knowing where else to start with the insane suggestion.

"Police if you're lucky," the man said.

"Ambulance if you're not," one of his colleagues chimed in. The others all laughed.

Damian glanced at the word cloud. *Deer* was now the largest word, followed by *stupid* and *die*. He couldn't even spot the words *peanut butter* or *dog*.

"What's the point of even wearing a costume when it's first person?" he complained. "No one will see it."

Curtis was quietly pleased that Damian was picking out specific issues with the idea rather than stubbornly rejecting it outright.

A VIP commenter than posted a message which caught Damian's eye. "Exactly," Damian said. "See, look at what this guy Realest_Rocco just said: *It's too dark to see the suit anyway, and that means it's too dark to see anything... which means it's not safe. And what's the point of getting killed doing a stunt that's not even funny?*"

"The formal vote is under way," one of the comedians said.

Their voices were all merging into one to the extent that Damian didn't know which one was speaking. Not that it mattered, he reflected, given that Curtis was feeding them the important lines anyway.

The same man continued: "And besides, deer get hit in the daytime, too. Watch this."

SycaCity then disappeared from Damian's wall, replaced by a compilation video called *Cars Vs Deer*.

Damian watched for a few seconds until the first stationary deer felt the crushing impact of a speeding vehicle. His eyes then looked away from the screen and landed on the newly appeared live poll. The "Deer" option had already pulled into the lead. A few comments along the lines of *"is he seriously going to do this? Surely not..."* appeared at the top of the chatbox, but such doubtful sentiments hadn't so far translated into votes.

"I'm not doing it," Damian typed, the words visible only to Curtis.

"This is it, man," the reply came quickly. "Make or break. Time to man up."

With no idea what else to do, Damian addressed his entire viewership out loud: "I seriously don't want to do this. Please... vote for peanut butter. If you all vote for peanut butter, I'll do two extra stunts tomorrow. I promise! They'll be really good ones."

Damian minimised his private conversation with Curtis and focused entirely on the live vote. To his delight, peanut butter began to pull into a lead that looked more insurmountable by the second. In the chatbox, countless viewers spoke of how glad they were that Damian wasn't going to have to do something so stupidly dangerous. He navigated back to his conversation with Curtis to send the word "*See*?", but Curtis had sent several angry messages since Damian last looked:

"Shut up, you idiot! We need something impactful!"

...

"Look what you've done."

...

"Dangerman? You call yourself Dangerman?!"

...

"Seriously, do you know what you've just done to us?"

Ultimately, it was the "us" that did it. As the voting drew to a close and peanut butter was pronounced the winner, Damian had an epiphany: Curtis, who was supposed to have his back, cared less about his safety than did the masses of random viewers who had supposedly tuned in to see him get hurt.

"I'm going to the bathroom," Damian announced to his viewers. "Don't worry, I'll be back in a minute. And thanks for the vote."

Damian's guest stars assured the audience that they weren't going anywhere and would keep talking over the now full-screen footage of their cooperative SycaCity game, which had returned to view now that the Cars vs Deer video was no longer relevant.

Inside his bathroom, Damian entered his security code on the invisible keypad. This blocked all Star's Eye View related activity and would continue to do so until his daily allowance of private time expired or until he entered the code again to resume broadcasting — whichever came first.

"You care less about me than these random commenters do," Damian yelled, voicing his earlier thoughts now that he knew only Curtis could hear. "Look at the vote: these people don't want to see an *actual* car crash! You're the only one who did."

Unapologetic, Curtis held his ground. "I was looking out for you! I was looking out for *us*. I just heard they've calmed Trixi down and she's going back online right now. That was our one chance, and you killed it. You really screwed us over, man. You really fu—"

"Shut up," Damian snapped.

"Who the hell are you talking to?" Curtis shot back. "Who got you here, you freak? Me!"

"And who's *keeping* me here? Who's the one doing the stunts? Which one of us has crushed toes and which one of us is counting the money for doing nothing?"

"Doing nothing?"

"What do you do that no one else could?" Damian asked. "In fact, you know what? Don't even answer. You're fired."

"I'm *what*?"

Damian gestured into his palm and selected the menu option to connect to someone at Sycamore HQ. He muted Curtis, requested to be put through to the SycaStar division, and asked the man on the other end of the line to remove Curtis as his rep with immediate effect. Damian confirmed that he understood such a decision was non-reversible.

"A new rep will be appointed as soon as possible," the man said. "In the meantime, your standby rep, Simone, will take charge."

Damian knew Simone from one day the previous week when Curtis had been ill and unable to perform his rep duties. She had seemed amiable enough.

"Hi Damian," she now said, speaking out loud to save time. "I'm super excited to be working with you again, but I think you should get back to the viewers. Don't you?"

"What did you think about the deer thing?" Damian asked.

After some pensive hesitation, Simone replied: "Anything which risks incapacitation should probably be avoided."

It was noncommittal and hardly sentimental, but Damian accepted the answer. "Okay," he said. "I'll get back to the viewers."

"Wait!" Simone yelled.

"Yeah?"

"May I suggest you wear the flesh-tone noseplugs which were delivered yesterday?"

Damian looked to the side of his sink, at the noseplugs he had been given the previous morning in case a stunt which involved him washing his face with toilet water had won its vote.

"Thanks," Damian said. He inserted the noseplugs and entered the code to resume his live visual stream.

"Jesus, Damian," one of the guest stars said. "I can smell that from here!"

"Very good," Damian replied. He noticed that his viewership had stabilised only slightly below its pre-drama peak; with Trixilicious back online and apparently maintaining a facade of business-as-usual, everything was reverting to normal.

The word cloud in Damian's chat box looked exactly as it should have before the kind of stunt he was about to perform: words like *gross, sick, disgusting* and *hilarious* now dominated.

Damian walked into his kitchen, hobbling noticeably as he tried to avoid placing too much weight on his injured foot. He opened his cupboard and reached for an unopened jar of smooth peanut butter.

"Dogs prefer the chunky kind," one of the guest stars offered, speaking his own thoughts now that Curtis the control freak was out of the picture.

"We could have a vote," Damian suggested. "I don't have chunky, but I could buy some."

All three of the night's guest stars vocally supported the notion of a vote, understanding perfectly well that interactivity was a core component of Star's Eye View.

Business as usual, Damian thought, smiling broadly as it dawned on him that he was free from Curtis and his sadism and now in control of his own channel.

The cumulative viewership figure crept back past 2.6 million and inched closer by the second towards yet another personal best.

"Okay," said Damian Dangerman, addressing his legion of loyal viewers. "Vote *smooth* or *chunky…*"

EIGHT

David

"Welcome to the new-look *This Week On Sycamore*," Kate Pinewood beamed into the camera from her crescent-shaped interview couch. "As you can see, I'm joined today by the man of the moment: viral sensation David Brown."

David nodded slightly. It was more than a slight stretch to describe this accidentally famous 14-year-old boy as a man, and the pressure of the moment appeared to have rendered his two hours of rehearsals worthless.

Although Kate had no prior experience as an interviewer, she sensed David's unease and quickly moved on with her lines in an effort to avoid too much dead air. And although this episode wasn't being broadcast live, Kate knew that her hopes of *future* episodes airing live — which she had suggested as a means of ensuring even greater viewing figures — depended entirely on how smoothly her first interview segment went. Kate's skill as a presenter was not in question, but she knew that Isaiah Amos would be watching like a hawk to gauge her ability as an interviewer.

"Your one-punch knockout of a schoolyard tormenter has already been watched and rewatched by more consumers than any other clip in *This Week On Sycamore* history," Kate continued, turning directly towards David. "But before we get onto the aftermath, I have to ask: how much did that punch hurt your fist?"

The cue overlaid in David's vision told him to laugh and shake his head, just like he had practised a dozen times. He sat perfectly still; expressionless.

"It sure *looked* like it hurt?" Kate prodded, inflecting the sentence into a question while making a laudable effort to hide her impatience with David's stage-fright.

David broke eye contact with Kate and subtly performed a series of quick gestures in his palm.

In search of assistance, Kate glanced at some of the crew behind the camera. Her focus was then abruptly broken by a pop-up notification of a newly received text message from David Brown.

Kate saw a poorly hidden grin spreading across David's face, which told her that something more troubling than stage-fright lay behind his silence. When she clicked to open the message, a single line of text confirmed her fears:

"Okay, Kate. Here's what's going to happen…"

~

If David Brown had his way, Kate Pinewood was about to suffer the same fate as Dr Norman McGill, the psychologist who David had recently caught betting on greyhound racing while he was supposed to have been listening to David's painful-to-share thoughts.

This evidence of negligence, gleaned from free trials of powerful Sycamore apps, had given David sufficient leverage to not only blackmail Dr McGill into sugar-coating his evaluation but also to directly extort a moderate sum of money.

This success highlighted the potential of Sycamore's mountains of data so strongly in David's eyes that he had since used his ill-gotten funds to buy full access to the same apps he'd used so profitably against Dr McGill. David saw this expenditure as a capital investment and fully expected it to pay for itself tenfold by allowing him to similarly extort other carefully chosen targets.

While in the process of scouting potential targets, David had received an unexpected invitation to appear alongside Kate Pinewood for a special interview on her immensely popular weekly show. Immediately, he began to dig.

Kate's fame made her the perfect target; as well as being extremely image-conscious, she was becoming increasingly wealthy as her stock rose in tandem with *This Week On Sycamore*'s viewership. She had a lot to lose and didn't strike David as someone likely to risk embarrassment over a sum of money which would barely make a dent in her balance.

Now, as Kate stared at David in confused anticipation of what would follow his apparent set-up for some kind of power play, David stared at a collage of the chat logs and images he had put together to ensure Kate's obedience. Given that the "dirt" he'd managed to find in the last seven days was relatively banal, his hopes rested on the assumption that Kate would rather make a small payment than risk taking even the slightest hit to her carefully cultivated public image.

"You're going to click the button to authorise this payment," David demanded in his second text message, "or I'm going to click the button to publish this dossier."

Kate's expression changed in an instant as a folder full of once-private photos and chat logs appeared in her vision. The photos were risqué if not graphic, but Kate's attention quickly fell on a chat log in which she described Isaiah Amos as "an egomaniacal creep." While the public's five-minute attention span would ensure that her public image could recover from the photos being leaked, Kate knew that Amos bore grudges like no one else and that her career would be over the second he saw her comments.

Kate was stunned. The only consolation she could draw was that the relatively mild nature of the leak David was threatening hinted that her account hadn't been compromised; if it *had*, she figured, he would've had a whole lot more.

The way David had actually obtained the data was more straightforward than Kate could have imagined: the other party in her discussion about Amos, like the recipient of her photos, had lazily left their privacy options on the extremely liberal default settings; settings which enabled any would-be snooper with sufficient funds to access another consumer's recent Forest conversations so long as a direct Forest connection existed between the snooper and the consumer. The potential sticking point in David's plan had been his need to establish such a connection, but his recent viral notoriety meant that everyone was keen to count him among their Forest friends. Kate's own privacy settings offered no protection against snoopers once her messages and photos reached their recipients.

After closing the evidence folder and firing a hate-filled glance in David's direction, Kate turned back towards her camera crew and production assistants. "I think some of these lights might be too bright for David's eyes," she said, playing it cool. "They're annoying *me,* and I'm used to it. Can someone bring him a glass of water, too? We'll pick up again in a few minutes."

Kate's eyes then glazed over once again as she focused on something in her Seed's menu. David watched optimistically, assuming that she was preparing to authorise the payment he had requested in exchange for not leaking her private files.

Optimism turned to impatience as David's glass of water arrived and Kate still hadn't made the payment. He began to wonder what she was doing.

"Uh, Miss Pinewood," said the man who delivered the water. "I don't mean to rush you, but we are working to a tight schedule. Are the lights okay now?"

"Perfect," Kate said with a satisfied smile. "*Everything* is perfect now." She then furtively swiped four fingers towards David, delivering two simple screenshots which caused his entire body to slump in defeat as a painful and sudden realisation dawned:

He had brought a knife to a gunfight.

Unbeknownst to David, Kate and two of her senior production assistants had been granted full read-only access to his Sycamore account in order to enable them to prepare for the interview.

Kate had chosen to leave the research and planning to her assistants, but their presence behind the camera had reminded her at the crucial moment that she still had access to David's account.

She went to the most obvious place first: his recent search history inside Sycamore's universal video streaming app. The first page of results provided more ready-made ammunition than she would need to convince David that any tit-for-tat leaks would be far more damaging for him than they would for her.

In case the screenshot of David's search history wouldn't be enough, Kate quickly navigated into his Relive app to see which vista recordings he had recently rewatched. She snapped a screenshot of one recording in which his eyes lecherously lingered on a girl the app conveniently identified as his 16-year-old cousin Nelle.

"Give me another two minutes and I'll find something worse," Kate typed.

David's expression left no doubt that he had already surrendered.

"Let's go from exactly where we left off," Kate said chirpily, addressing her crew and then smiling at David as though nothing had happened. "Before we get on to the aftermath, I have to ask: how much did that punch hurt your fist?"

This time, thoroughly humbled, David followed his cue. Since the half-heartedness of his laughter could be naturally attributed to nerves rather than the humbling he had just experienced, Kate saw no need for a second take.

The rest of the brief interview passed without a hitch. Kate sent David on his way as soon as the segment was recorded, keen to get him out of her sight.

"I'll be watching you," she quietly lied as they shook hands, knowing full well that he would never try to mess with her again.

After filming the rest of the episode in one flawless take, Kate gathered her things and headed for the exit. As soon as she pressed the downward-pointing arrow to call the elevator to her 19th floor base, a familiar voice spoke directly into Kate's in-earphones.

"No," the man said, unmistakably Amos. "You're going up."

Kate was startled; not by being directly addressed by Amos, which she had grown used to in light of their many discussions about *This Week On Sycamore*'s overall direction, but rather by the suddenness of his orders and the fact that he had evidently been watching her. "Your office?" she asked, trying to regain her composure.

"We have much to discuss," Amos replied in the affirmative. He then cut off their direct voice chat and waited patiently for Kate outside the elevator on the expansive 22nd floor he called his office.

Kate's thoughts jumped around like a pinball as she wondered what she had done wrong. Had Amos heard reports of a lacklustre interview from one of the camera crew? Had she blown her one chance? The first words she heard when the elevator door opened did little to assuage these concerns.

"I don't think this current arrangement is going to get the best out of you," Amos said. "This arrangement with you running the show and interviewing guests… I just don't think it's playing to your strengths."

Kate knew better than to argue and was grateful that Amos was being diplomatic in his analysis. "So I'll go back to just introducing the clips?" she asked, hoping against hope that this role — the source of her fame — wouldn't also be snatched from her grasp.

Amos shook his head.

"You're letting me go?" Kate gasped. "Firing me?"

"Kate, if you would listen to what—"

With nothing left to lose, Kate exploded into a multi-sentence rant about how Amos had never appreciated how much of *This Week On Sycamore*'s success was down to her and how he would never find someone to fill her shoes.

Amos said nothing while Kate vented.

"Why are you smiling?" she snapped.

"I'm offering you a promotion, Kate. A *big* one. I watched the interview with that troublemaker and I saw how you handled him."

"Watched it where? It hasn't aired yet and you weren't there."

"I was watching through your eyes," Amos said, like it was the most ordinary thing in the world. "Don't worry about the 'egomaniacal creep' comment, by the way; if I reacted to every private quip my employees make behind my back, this place would be empty! Anyway… I saw the boy's threats and I saw how you reacted. That's when it clicked: your talents are wasted downstairs. Utterly wasted."

Kate stayed quiet, surprised by his relaxed reaction to the insult.

"I need someone I can trust, Kate. Since everything that happened with Terrance, I've needed someone I can trust to disarm troublemakers. Your dignified silence after Kurt exposed your true role at the Talent Search tells me that you can be trusted, and the way you so quickly knew exactly what kind of threat the boy would respond to tells me that you can perform the job I'm offering."

"And to be totally clear about what that job *is*…?"

"If an individual is causing trouble or threatening to do so — either against one of our systems or one of our employees — we sometimes need human intervention," Amos explained.

"A scalpel is preferable to a sledgehammer when we're dealing with individuals motivated by chaos. Account suspension offers no real threat to grudge-bearers whose faculties have abandoned them. Threats against their reputations are far more effective. Terrance used to handle this; whenever threats were flagged, he would find something embarrassing enough to disarm them. No one man can fully replace Terrance — or woman, of course — but you can fill this particular void. What do you say?"

"Don't we have a security app that automatically detects sensitive data which could be used for blackmail? Would it not be easier to reconfigure the app to display the data and tell the consumer it will be published unless they cease whatever they're doing?"

Amos nodded, again impressed by Kate's thinking. "We already do that. But Terrance was an independent thinker and any app can only be as incisive as the book-smart people who wrote it. Terrance knew how to hit troublemakers where it hurt, and you just showed that you have the same instinct."

Kate mulled over the offer.

"Do you know how many people have been on this floor?" Amos asked, catching her off guard with the unexpected question.

She shook her head.

"Nine, including the two of us. The last first-time visitor was Kurt."

Kate read between the lines: this wasn't just an offer of a promotion, it was an invitation into the inner circle.

"There's no shame in enjoying fame," Amos said, correctly deducing that Kate, while flattered and enticed, was loath to give up her highly visible position as the star of *This Week On Sycamore*. "But while fame is a valid pursuit, it's important to remember that fame is a means to an end. That end is power, Kate... and I'm offering you more of it than you could ever imagine."

Kate shifted uneasily and looked out of Amos's endless window, gazing down at the street below.

"You see that guy in front of the SycaPlex?" Amos said. "In the red coat."

"What about him?"

Amos answered by swiping his fingers towards the window, creating a huge virtual screen which blocked Kate's view of the ground.

After a few short seconds, Kate realised that the first-person footage before her eyes was a live stream of Red Coat's vista. She turned to Amos in amazement.

He tilted his head towards the screen, sending her attention back to it. With a few more taps of his finger, Amos then brought up Red Coat's main menu, displaying unimpeded access to all of the innocent man's data.

"You're saying I could do that with *anyone's* account?" Kate asked. "Without them even knowing?"

Amos nodded proudly as he swept away the virtual screen. "Aside from any Sycamore employee with higher security clearance than your own, that is. To be clear: I will expect swift and decisive results whenever potential troublemakers are detected and brought to your attention. My tools and your instincts can become a potent combination. But outside of work hours, I don't care what else you do with these tools. As long as it doesn't interfere with your work, you can snoop on whoever you want. Perks of the job," he said with a demonic grin.

"You just said that as long as I do my job when you need me to, it doesn't matter what I do the rest of the time... correct?"

"Indeed."

"Then I want to keep presenting the show," Kate said in a firm and assured tone. "I can do it in one shoot. It will only take a few hours per week, and we can shoot in the middle of the night if we have to."

Amos understood that, for some, fame was a psychological

need independent of power. He didn't understand *why*, but he understood that it was. Kate Pinewood was a perfect SycAmbassador who would have been difficult to adequately replace, and Amos couldn't disagree that a few hours per week would be manageable.

"Kate," he whispered, placing a cold hand on her exposed shoulder as he stood beside her at the window and gazed down at his world. "If you're happy, I'm happy."

NINE

Steve

As a harsh alarm signalled the beginning of 'Skinny' Steve Keller's workday, he and his fellow SDU inmates rose from their low dining benches. The day had started well for Steve, who had felt refreshed by a good night's sleep and a hot shower even before the varied delights of an all-you-can-eat SDU breakfast.

Steve walked under the large sign marked "Canteen (D Ward)" and gestured in his palm to pull up the shortest route to the unfamiliar location he had been assigned to for the day. Having initially believed that his was simply the fourth of however many alphabetically ordered wards there were, Steve now knew that the D stood for Destitute. Destitute inmates comprised slightly over one-third of an average Secure Dependency Unit's population, and Steve's Unit was perfectly typical in this regard.

Everyone around Steve wore identically styled clothing with the only difference being the colour of their T-shirts, all of which were plain aside from a large 'D' on the front and back. Blue was the most common colour, followed closely by grey and more distantly by white and green. Steve's colour — yellow — was rarer than all but one.

All of the men were clean-shaven and had been given

compulsory haircuts upon entry to the SDU. These haircuts were nothing like the near-scalpings often inflicted upon inmates in regular prisons, as Steve knew from previous personal experience, instead resembling the more attentive and expensive work of real commercial hairstylists. This distinction was one of many explained to Steve during a brief introductory video which insisted that the SDU's purpose was not to punish its inmates nor strip them of their humanity but rather to help them help themselves. There had been something about the inmates' work providing benefits to society before they re-emerged as full members, along with words like *symbiotic* and *synergistic*. Steve, thinking at the time that it was all talk, hadn't paid much attention. Now, though, he believed every word.

Much to Steve's confusion, the body language and facial expressions of the other men could best be summed up by a word that in no way mirrored his own feelings: miserable.

Steve simply couldn't understand why everyone looked so downtrodden. His bed was comfortable, the staff treated him with dignity, and his work was more than bearable. To him, the surrounding negativity bordered on ungratefulness. After mulling it over for several seconds, he ultimately assumed that the general glumness all around him must have been down to the SDU's strict "no visitors" rule. Though this rule didn't affect Steve, he could appreciate that it must have been eating away at the many husbands and fathers among his Destitute companions.

The only other strictly enforced rule within the SDU was the outright ban on work-related discussion. With wards assigned based on inmates' reason for admission rather than the kind of work they had been given, Steve had no idea what the vast majority of the men did all day. Having seen a handful of yellow-shirted men walking the quiet aisles near his own usual work booth — men from D Ward as well as others — Steve took their presence to mean that the shirt colours were related to work groupings.

Steve readily accepted the official reason for the ban on

work-related discussion: most men were involved in testing of some kind, whether that meant identifying software bugs or subjectively appraising new apps, and the integrity of such tests was dependent upon the testers going in with no preconceived notions. If one man knew what kind of exciting new app his workmate had been looking at the previous day, his own reactions would be spoiled and invalid.

A small handful of men had been disciplined for breaking this rule, and Steve had little sympathy. He knew that the integrity of testing was paramount to the SDU system; a system which was an undeniable win-win as Sycamore gained access to as many testers as it needed and the government saved untold amounts of money that would otherwise have been spent on conventional incarceration or welfare assistance. Steve's physical comfort within the SDU — something he had sorely lacked over his recent years on the street — was such a welcome respite that he bore no grudges towards Sycamore. His arrest for the "crime" of failing to pay his Movement Tax just 24 hours after being compulsorily seeded may have been an easy way for Sycamore to beef up the SDU's numbers, but Steve wouldn't have cared even had he reflected on this.

The SDU system was wholly privatised and subject to no real regulation, but Steve's experiences of public correctional facilities — particularly when considered in contrast to the SDU and its relative luxury — left him glad that the government was nowhere to be seen.

The nature of Steve's particular work further entrenched his faith in the stated justification for the ban on work-related discussion. Having been identified as unusually keen-eyed during his extensive pre-entry screening process, Steve had been put to work as a QA technician for Sycamore's Atmospherics department. This grand-sounding role essentially involved spotting tiny flaws in fully immersive previews of the kind of augmented overlays Sycamore used to spruce up public areas in sore need of a fresh lick of paint.

Thus far, Steve had spent each of his workdays in a quiet

and isolated booth, studiously analysing dozens of designs. Unlike the example used in the screening process, the designs Steve analysed were not littered with several small but deliberate errors; rather, these designs had already been carefully checked by the well-paid Atmospherics team in Sycamore HQ's basement Studio and were passed over to Steve and others like him for one final lookover.

Designs ranged from six-inch paint repairs to miles-long floral designs intended to brighten up the tired-looking edges of busy roadways. Those designs which fell on the small and simple end of the spectrum rarely contained any flaws for Steve to flag up; so much so, he had now taken to skimming such designs only briefly and instead focusing on those large enough for the flaws to blend in and go unseen by Sycamore's staff.

For every confirmed flaw that Steve spotted, he received a supposedly financial reward in the form of entertainment credits to spend in the SycaStore. The judge who sentenced Steve to an SDU stay informed him that a man in his position — with no outstanding debts but no assets to speak of — could expect to take three years to earn sufficient actual money to ensure he would be able to provide for himself in the outside world. The fact that their reward for good work was having SycaStore credit added to their accounts, as opposed to real money, angered most inmates by virtue of eliminating their ability to hasten their exits. Steve, however, was wholly content where he was.

The previous day had been Steve's most successful yet as he identified an error on a row of flowerbeds which would have been repeated 28 times along a seven-mile stretch of road. Steve at first drew upon his work as a home decorator; specifically utilising his experience of applying wallpaper with the kind of complex repeating patterns favoured by some wealthy homeowners. The problem with the seven-mile flowerbed design boiled down to a glaring inconsistency in the colour saturation of a blue flower rather than any problem at the point where the end of each quarter-mile stretch joined the beginning of the next, but Steve's identification of 28 errors in one fell swoop didn't go unnoticed by his supervisors. On top of the usual SycaStore credits, received in this case for all 28 single instances of the same error, Steve received a notice that he would be permitted to work outside for the rest of the week.

When the directions in Steve's UltraLenses led him to a previously unexplored courtyard, the sounds of chirping birds and a light breeze buffeting a fledgling tree engulfed him in a feeling of serenity. His eyes quickly adjusted to the natural light as he left the dimly lit corridor and spotted another man entering the courtyard from a door on the other side. This man, like Steve, wore a yellow T-shirt. But where Steve's yellow T-shirt was emblazoned with a D, this man's was emblazoned with an A.

The man's hollow stare and razor-sharp cheekbones left Steve in little doubt that A stood for Addict.

"Hey," the man said as their eyes met.

Steve's UltraLenses identified the man as Frank Vorhees, a 36-year-old SDU resident.

Frank walked towards one of the five empty chairs in the centre of the courtyard. He moved with purpose and showed no signs of ill health apart from the visible signs of previous malnourishment. As far as Steve could tell, it looked liked Frank's recovery was going well.

"Good morning," Steve replied. He made his way to the seat singled out by an arrow in his vista as the correct one.

"It's Destitute, right?" Frank asked. "The D?"

Steve nodded. "Addict?"

Frank nodded in return and smiled warmly. "This place is the best thing that ever happened to me."

~

Steve got to work on his latest assignment: an intricate clean up of a very old-fashioned cobbled road on what seemed to be a relatively low-income residential street, judging by what he could see through the windows. To his mild frustration, Steve couldn't see any flaws.

Before long, frustration turned to annoyance. Steve wasn't annoyed by the irresponsible decision to digitally mask the degrading brickwork rather than to fix it; no... rather than being annoyed by the fact that this job had been done, Steve was annoyed that it had been done so well. Twenty minutes which felt more like twenty hours passed before he finally expressed his annoyance by sighing.

"Can you not find anything, either?" Frank said, catching Steve off guard.

"Huh?" Steve asked. He quickly gestured into his palm to exit full immersion and turned towards Frank.

"How many flaws did you find in the design?"

"None," Steve said. He didn't add the word *yet*; in his mind, that would have been unjustifiably optimistic.

Frank's eyes narrowed. "Did they have you looking at flower beds? A really long line of flower beds at the side of the highway?"

"I did that yesterday," Steve said. "Today it was—"

"A cobbled street," Frank interrupted. It wasn't a question. "No wonder we can't find anything!"

Steve thought in silence for a few seconds. He couldn't decide whether someone had made an error in assigning their designs or whether he and Frank had deliberately been tasked with double-checking each other's previous work.

"How are we supposed to get rewards for finding flaws if there are no flaws to find?" Frank went on, his tone growing angrier. "I'm going to find Mitch Dallas and ask what's going on."

Steve gulped. "You think that's a good idea?"

Frank dismissed Steve's concerns with a confident nod. "If we go together to ask if this was supposed to happen, that will show we actually care about the work; that we're not just phoning it in."

"It'll show that we've being talking about work," Steve said. "That's what it'll show! And you know the rules on that."

"Those rules mean don't talk to other *groups* about the kind of work you do. There's nothing about talking within your own group."

As far as Steve knew, this distinction had no basis in reality. His facial expression reflected his misgivings.

"Look, man..." Frank said, rising to his feet. "I'm going to talk to Dallas. He'll know we've been talking about work, because how else would I know what work you did yesterday? So if you don't come with me, it's probably going to look bad for you."

Steve stood up without speaking, as angry at himself for sighing as he was at Frank for being so heedless and manipulative. The men walked inside, via the door on Frank's side of the courtyard, and silently continued along the corridor towards their destination.

Mitch Dallas, the SDU's Chief Liaison Officer, was responsible for acting as something of a bridge between inmates and the Unit's unseen management. Widely known as Dallas, he was best known to most inmates as the man who featured in the Q&A videos available via their Seeds. Dallas had also hosted what he called a settling-in tour for Steve and the rest of the previous week's intake, during which Steve had quickly come to like him. The man had an easy way about him, so Steve hadn't been surprised to learn that he previously worked as a high school principal.

Sooner than he expected, Steve found himself outside a door marked "CLO".

Frank stepped forward and knocked three times.

"Gentleman," Dallas said, half cordial and half confused. "What can I help you with?"

Frank spat out his question as quickly as he could, in a manner that Steve couldn't help but consider needlessly brusque.

Dallas gestured into his palm and for several seconds

displayed the unmistakably distant gaze of someone looking at something that wasn't really there. "The logs say it was supposed to happen," he eventually said, returning to focus. "Yes… each of you was definitely supposed to see the same design that the other saw yesterday. We appreciate your dedication to efficiency, but for future reference: please remember that work-related discussions is prohibited. In this instance, given your unusual proximity during the work session and the unusual specifics of that session, no further action will be taken."

"So you won't make sure this doesn't happen again?" Frank asked, surprised that Dallas seemed to have expected him to be happy that no action would be taken. "Because we're both good at what we do, so if you're going to keep giving us designs that the other one has already checked, how the hell are we supposed to earn more entertainment credits and outdoor work sessions?"

A voice came from behind Steve and Frank. "Entertainment credits?" it asked, dumbfounded. "Outdoor work sessions?"

Steve turned to see two men, both wearing red shirts. He recognised one of them from D Ward. The other man's red shirt was marked with an A, making the pair an inversion of Steve and Frank.

"What the hell are they talking about?" the same man asked, aiming his furious question squarely at Dallas. "What kind of work are these guys doing?"

Dallas gestured in his palm and spoke quietly: "Immediate backup required. Repeat, immediate backup required."

Steve knew that red shirts were reserved for Illiterates. These were men with so little experience of pre-Sycamore technologies that the initial screening process proved basic touch gestures to be beyond them, along with the performing of core human tasks such as typing efficiently or attaching files to messages. The time it would have taken to train such men to a level of basic proficiency in any useful task far outweighed the value of doing so, leaving them in the unenviable position of performing the least desirable tasks in the SDU. Steve often saw red-shirted inmates cleaning toilets or serving meals, but he had no idea where these tasks fell on the undesirability spectrum.

But now, just a few feet from two incensed-looking Illiterates, Steve saw that both had small scars on their foreheads. He looked into his own left hand, confirming where he recognised the shape of the scars from.

The Illiterate who had so far been quiet then exploded with rage, his words confirming Steve's suspicions: "You're putting chips in our goddamn foreheads and using us to test mental torture techniques, and these guys are—"

"It's not *torture,*" Dallas said, more derisively than defensively.

"Bombarding us with sounds of screams and pictures of horrible crap we can't look away from, all to see how we react… that's not torture? Showing one inmate a fake video of his family being killed by another inmate, just to see how far he'll go to get his hands on him… that's not messed up? And don't think we don't know about Rogers. Don't think he didn't tell us about the sleep deprivation tests you'd been doing on him for two weeks, flashing lights in his eyes all night and whatever else you were doing! Don't think we don't know that's why he did it!"

Steve's mind put pieces of a puzzle together, recalling rumours from two days earlier that an Illiterate in F Ward had thrown himself from a third-floor balcony. The news that he'd done so after prolonged and deliberate "sleep deprivation tests", presumably conducted by SDU staff, added a horrific new dimension to an already tragic tale.

As distant footsteps grew suddenly nearer, Dallas looked directly at Steve and pulled a finger across his own lips in an easily understood gesture.

Steve then turned to his right, where he spotted two Sycamore agents running along the corridor having sprinted from the Unit's front desk where they had been in the process of delivering a fresh batch of D Ward inmates. Immediately, Steve recognised one of the men as Rocco Miller, the young man who had stood trial at the same time as him and who had escaped an SDU stay by agreeing — at Steve's suggestion — to assume a role as a Movement Tax Enforcer.

"You called for backup?" Rocco asked, focusing on Dallas after briefly glancing at the four inmates. He didn't recognise Steve, which was hardly surprising given the rapid transformation in Steve's appearance that had occurred since his arrival in the Unit.

"These two Illiterates have become aware of the kind of work undertaken by the Atmospherics QA team. Needless to say, if the extent of the disparity between the daily activities of skilled workers and Illiterates became common knowledge among the rest of the Illiterates..." Dallas trailed off.

"Understood," the taller agent said. He cuffed one of the Illiterates while Rocco cuffed the other. "And what about these two?"

Dallas glanced between Steve and Frank. "There's no further problem," he then said to the agent. "One group of workers doesn't tend to mind when they find out that another group's work is more difficult."

"Work?" Frank blurted out. "Sleep deprivation and fake videos of their families being killed? Since when the hell is that work?"

"This one will have to go, too," Dallas said flatly.

Rocco, effortlessly though somewhat reluctantly, restrained Frank's flailing arms and cuffed him along with the Illiterates.

"And you're sure that's all, Mr Dallas?" the other agent asked.

Dallas looked deeply into Steve's eyes for several seconds; long enough to be sure Steve understood that the smart move was keeping his mouth shut. "That's all," he decided.

The agents then set off in the direction they'd come, with Frank calling Steve all the names under the sun as he was dragged away. Dallas tilted his head to dismiss Steve without speaking.

Steve left without hesitation.

"Oh, Mr Keller," Dallas called. "One thing."

Steve stopped and turned round. "Uh, yes, Mr Dallas?"

"I'll see to it that some extra entertainment credits are added to your account. For your… discretion. And please: don't hesitate to raise any further questions you might have about your work. Identifying flaws in the Atmospherics department's overlays is a crucial task."

Steve nodded and set off again. He soon re-entered the now empty courtyard and retook his seat to study some more designs.

Three more years, he thought to himself as an unfamiliar digitally repainted parking lot appeared in his vision.

Three… more… years…

TEN

Kayla

Kayla Monroe sat quietly at her desk, passing the time during a particularly soul-crushing chemistry class in the best way she knew: by watching and re-watching footage of her recent and frequent attempts to disrupt Sycamore's systems.

The serious hand injury which had delayed Kayla's seeding meant that these systems were far newer to her than they were to the rest of her classmates, but she had spent her first four days as a fully fledged member of Sycamore's brave new world making up for lost time and was now as familiar with the intricacies as anyone.

Unlike most young consumers in Kayla's position would have, however, she hadn't looked forward to her eventual seeding with glee. On the contrary, Kayla had dreaded her introduction to the hyper-connected network. The idea of her many friends and acquaintances knowing where she was at all times was troubling enough, but the idea of a corporation knowing every little thing she did and using that knowledge to monetise every little aspect of her existence…

In the first few hours, Kayla found herself surprised to be enjoying the ease of communication that came with everyone being permanently connected to the same social network under their real name, as well as the undeniably enticing mountain of freemium games which already made excellent and innovative use of the Seed-and-UltraLenses combo. But once those few hours passed and the system began to learn and predict Kayla's consumer behaviour, the ads arrived.

Even had she felt no qualms about privacy or anything else, the ads would have been enough to turn Kayla against Sycamore. Her friend and neighbour Dexter had mentioned the invasiveness and near-ubiquity of the ad placements, but the *extent* of those placements truly had to be seen to be believed.

Since then, Kayla had been doing her best to mess with the system. Her early efforts involved downloading a huge number of free apps and huge quantities of free entertainment content, with the intent of confusing the system over which type of content it should recommend next. After that, she attempted to pollute her Consumer Interest Profile at Tasmart Online by adding incongruent item combinations to her wish-list: artificial grass and an industrial-sized bottle of lawn-feed; electronic candles and a value pack of matches; and whatever other trivial examples entered her mind. To Kayla's childish delight, ad placements for Tasmart Online products and SycaStore entertainment content soon became erratic and anything but targeted.

Boosted by her early success, Kayla invested a few hours in becoming more familiar with the workings of Sycamore's ad-placement algorithms. Information on most kinds of ad targeting and delivery was openly available in the form of informational videos filmed inside Sycamore HQ. These videos boasted of the infallibility of the algorithms, which were "informed by innumerable variables across a broad spectrum of consumer behaviour." Through a cloud of such meaningless verbiage, Kayla learned about the so-called Triangle ads: expensive ads that were served at opportune moments based on a consumer's identity, interest, and location.

Kayla, armed with this knowledge, immediately took to doing things like standing in the mall's food court and proclaiming out loud: "I sure could go for a burger right now. If only there was somewhere close..."

A perfectly targeted Triangle ad would then be served following an automatic bidding contest between rival fast-food outlets. In her enjoyment of these moments, Kayla failed to consider that all the expensive ad placements were really doing was lining Sycamore's pockets.

Kayla's other favourite hobby — pestering Sycamore's live video help assistants with nonsensical problems — provided most of the viewing material which saw her through boring classes. Watching the assistants try to explain the root of her problems without calling her stupid provided hours of entertainment. Kayla's favourite problem was the one which caused her entire vision to turn brown, at which point she would initiate a video help request to inform an assistant that something was wrong with her UltraLenses. Sometimes the overworked help assistants would take several minutes to notice the cause and suggest the remedy: "Take off your sunglasses."

Because she knew that the help assistants were just doing their jobs, Kayla didn't seek to embarrass them publicly by sharing any of their confused replies online. The only person she ever showed was Dexter, who wasn't exactly in favour of messing with the system but wouldn't object as long as Kayla didn't do anything crazy. He had known her long enough to know that she wasn't going to do nothing, so he considered it better for her mind to be amused by something relatively trivial like this than for it to be bored and free to think of something worse.

Ever since they were young children heartbroken at being split up when Kayla started school and Dexter was stuck at home, she had always been the live-wire of the duo. Kayla was at least less outwardly destructive now than she had been during a spell several years earlier which she now looked back on as her "cry for attention" phase, which ended abruptly when she caused thousands of dollars of damage by deliberately clogging a school drainpipe with paint. Knowing that

Kayla had been one incident away from serious trouble both at home and at school, and despite her initial protests, Dexter took the fall for this prank. Kayla promised him she would never do anything like that again, and a matter-of-fact promise to Dexter meant a lot more than the doe-eyed kind that could so effectively disarm her parents and school administrators.

Dexter had previously thought that the night before Kayla's belated seeding would be her last rebellious fling, when she gave him the chance for one more night of fun and he took it by scrawling "Sycamore Sucks" on a wall that would be passed by hundreds of consumers every day but seen by none thanks to the overlay work of Sycamore's Atmospherics department. That night ended with Kayla vowing to use her compulsory participation in Sycamore's world as a means to disrupt it, so Dexter had ultimately been relieved that her actions thus far had been relatively harmless.

The promise of staying out of major trouble which Kayla had made to Dexter was the reason for the candid words she now spoke in the lunch hall after showing him her latest sunglasses-based prank call to live help: "I have an idea for something bigger. Seriously, Dex… it's too good not to do."

He sighed. "Kayla…"

"I know, I know. But at least hear me out, okay? If you can listen to this idea and tell me it's not brilliant, I'll forget all about it. Deal?"

Dexter scanned the bustling lunch hall for prying eyes and ears.

"It's safe to talk," Kayla said. "It's not like anyone is listening…"

~

In a large and tastefully arranged office in Sycamore HQ, Kate Pinewood glanced over her latest list of potential troublemakers. The system delivered such a list three times per day, and most of the names she saw were already under investigation.

One of the new names immediately jumped out at Kate thanks to the three flags beside it: Kayla Monroe.

Since assuming Terrance Minion's old duty of ensuring consumer compliance, Kate had personally intervened on a handful of occasions when a troublemaking consumer had two flags. She had never before seen anyone with *three* flags.

Kate clicked to see further details of Kayla Monroe's suspected misdeeds. Abuse-detection algorithms in the Data Integrity department had flagged up Kayla's account following an exceptional number of SycaStore downloads, for erratic search and browsing patterns, and for frequent and often lengthy conversations with live help assistants. The thresholds for flags in each of these areas were so high that it was almost unheard of for any consumer's regular usage to be flagged up, regardless of how untypical that user's own definition of regular usage might have been.

One such flag indicated that deliberate misbehaviour was likely. Three flags removed all doubt.

As Kate delved deeper into Kayla Monroe's consumer profile, more warning signs emerged. None were more serious than the large red exclamation mark beside the clickable link to her advertising history. Kate noticed that Kayla had received an extraordinarily high number of Triangle ads — one of the most expensive kinds — and that her response rate was zero.

Though Kate was no advertising expert, she understood perfectly well that Triangle ads were so expensive because they were so effective. For someone to see as many such ads as Kayla had was anomalous; for someone to respond to none of them was dangerous. If the average sell-through rate of Triangle ads fell, so would the amount that advertisers were willing to pay for them. As such, an individual with an ad profile like Kayla Monroe's was a threat to the advertising revenue which had already come to be a vast and indispensable portion of Sycamore's income.

Having followed Kayla's live movements for several

minutes, Kate reacted with interest when she heard the suspect mention "an idea for something bigger."

At this point, with sufficient reason to think it necessary, Kate returned to Kayla's main consumer profile and clicked a link marked "BEGIN INTERVENTION".

~

"What's wrong?" Dexter asked, reacting to a sudden change in Kayla's expression.

Kayla said nothing as she read a four-line message which could have been summed up in four words: stop messing with us.

"Hello? Kayla? What's wrong?"

Kayla dismissed the message and refocused on Dexter. "Nothing important, just some old crap about my ad profile."

Dexter looked relieved. "So what's this idea you were going to tell me about?" he said, keen to put it to bed by hearing Kayla out and telling her that it wasn't brilliant.

"*Ugh…*"

"What?"

"Another message," Kayla groaned. "Some consumer services rep, I think. It looks like it was written by a human, anyway."

"What does it say?"

Kayla rose to her feet. "I'm going to the bathroom," she said. "Back in a sec."

~

"I'm not a consumer services rep," Kate Pinewood announced directly into Kayla's in-earphones.

Kayla continued walking until she was outside and alone. "So who are you?"

"Someone you should listen to," Kate said flatly. Had she known anything about Kayla beyond the system's one-size-fits-all metrics, she would have known that these words would only be taken as a challenge.

Typically for Kate, children were the easiest troublemakers to deal with; most exhibited a healthy fear of discipline which meant that the threat of a school suspension or even a mere call to their parents was enough to curb their misbehaviour. Unfortunately for Kate, Kayla Monroe was no such child.

"I've been scanning your profile," Kate said immediately after identifying herself as a Sycamore Compliance Officer. "Would you care to explain your persistent efforts to disrupt the function of advertising systems and your repeated time-wasting conversations with live help assistants?"

Kayla smirked. "Define explain."

"If you don't want this to escalate, I strongly suggest that you avoid repeating any of these actions and particularly that you abandon the notion of doing, quote, *something bigger*."

"Define escalate," Kayla challenged.

After a few seconds, Kayla found herself looking at a series of Forest posts she had made and photos she had posted in the last few days. The posts were private in nature.

"An escalation would begin with changes to the share settings on posts like these," Kate said, using the same tactics and the same detached voice she always did when dealing with the more hardheaded of consumers.

Kayla glanced over the posts. Upon deciding there was nothing *too* bad, and certainly nothing that wouldn't blow over in a few days, she gestured into her palm to make all of the posts public. "Now what?" she said.

Kate hesitated. All of the interventions she had performed so far, as well as the initial job-earning intervention she had made to disarm David Brown when he attempted to hijack an episode of *This Week On Sycamore*, had been far more straightforward than this. David and others like him had been motivated by clear-cut drivers like greed or anger or revenge and were thus rational in their approach. But Kayla Monroe, as Kate belatedly realised, was motivated by a driver altogether less rational: the pursuit of chaos and disruption for its own sake.

"I was in the news, you know," Kayla said, seizing her moment to pounce on Kate's impotence. "People know my face and feel sorry for me." She then looked down at her recently seeded left palm, still slightly scarred from the bite which had delayed the seeding in the first place. "How do you think this would look… a ruthless Sycamore worker blackmailing a poor kid who was finally able to get her seed last week after waiting so long? If you ever want to find out, I guess I could always publish this little chat, right?"

Kate frantically scanned through Kayla's Forest account for something else with blackmail potential, but she came up short. The girl had only been seeded for a few days and was smart enough to keep negative thoughts about others to herself, which deprived Kate of her most reliable form of ammunition. She could wipe this conversation from Kayla's history, of course, but it wouldn't be easy to fill the gap with something else and she had no doubt that the girl would insistently claim to have had her timeline disrupted. This risked breaching the first rule of Kate's job: don't make it worse. Whatever Kayla Monroe's "something bigger" idea was, Kate deemed it unlikely to cause more harm than that which would arise from pushing her any further; at least until further ammunition presented itself.

"I think there's been a misunderstanding here," Kate said, glad at least that the system automatically masked her voice so Kayla wouldn't know that she had just been threatened by none other than Kate Pinewood. She definitely seemed like the type who would brag about such a thing, Kate reflected.

"Good," Kayla said, more relieved than celebratory. "Now get the hell out of my timeline, you creep."

Kate retreated.

Kayla walked back inside and rejoined Dexter at their table in the lunch hall.

"You okay?" Dexter asked. "What was the message from the consumer rep about?"

Kayla dismissed his concerns with a quick shake of her head. "That? It was nothing. But anyway, about this idea I have..."

ELEVEN

Max

Getting robbed that night was the best thing that could have happened, Max Jasper thought to himself as he sat at the casino's plush bar.

The arrival of his fourth drink — spiced rum and lemonade, like the first three — marked the beginning of Max's fourth hour in the casino. In that time, his friend and accomplice Stavros had won the pair more money than either could typically earn in a week.

Before Max lost his old phone in a violent mugging, he and Stav had been focusing their energies on pool. But while Stav had shown promise and Max's pool-hacking app had proven the validity of their overall concept of covertly using imported UltraLenses to gain an insurmountable competitive advantage in high-stakes games of skill, it had since become abundantly apparent that poker was a more appropriate and more lucrative avenue.

Such was its relative simplicity, Max's poker-hacking app had taken no more than a few hours to throw together; a far cry from the 37 focused hours demanded by its pool-based predecessor. The pool app was as complicated to use as it had been difficult to create, requiring Stav — equipped with a shadily imported and fully hacked pair of UltraLenses — to subtly calibrate his Lenses to each table before he played on it. From a safe distance, Max had controlled the app and overlaid an ideal shot-line in Stav's vision. But even in the vast majority of instances when the angles were correct, success depended on the steadiness of Stav's arm.

The poker app, as well as assisting with a game in which Stav was already relatively accomplished, had no such drawbacks.

Right now, on the other side of the bustling casino, the app was running on autopilot in Stav's vision and giving him the maximum possible advantage over his unknowing rivals.

As soon as Stav looked at the cards he was holding, a percentage appeared in his vision to inform him of their probability of victory. This percentage updated on the flop and again on the turn and the river, should the hand go that far, as well as whenever Stav blinked twice to tell the app that one of his opponents had folded. On its own, this useful feature would have given Stav's chances a boost by cancelling out the mathematical knowledge of his more experienced opponents.

But Stav's real edge came from the app's *other* key feature: its ability to read his opponents' faces. Focusing on any opponent's face for longer than a second prompted his UltraLenses to annotate that face with countless arrows and markings, all of which gave an insight into the opponent's current mindset. The underlying technology was primarily used in commercial lie-detection software and had only recently been made available to the public with the launch of Sycamore's controversial *Reader* app. Just as Reader enabled any wealthy consumer on the other side of the Atlantic to use their UltraLenses to reveal their target's feelings via an instantaneous analysis of involuntary facial tics and ordinarily imperceptible muscle movements, Stav's app allowed him to judge — with incredible accuracy — which opponents were bluffing and which were trying to underplay the strength of their hands.

Max couldn't claim credit for creating the unofficial version of Reader, nor for developing the card-recognition technology or even the real-time probability calculator. But Max *could* claim credit for integrating it all into one self contained poker-hacking app which now allowed his intrepid ally to compete with prodigious hobbyists and hardened pros alike.

Tonight had been the app's biggest test so far, and Stav's biggest test to boot. Both were in the process of passing with flying colours.

Max took his drink to a quiet sofa and lifted his phone from his pocket to watch Stav play what would hopefully be the night's decisive hand. Max's phone, a like-for-like replacement for his Systelonik XK6 which had been stolen a week earlier, relayed live footage of Stav's vision as captured by his hacked UltraLenses. This gave Max an even better view than the handful of excited onlookers who were watching the climactic hand from the viewing area.

Play at Stav's table had proceeded more quickly than at the other three qualifying tables, meaning that whichever of its remaining two players came out on top would be the first to earn a free buy-in for the following night's high-stakes tournament. Max had already guaranteed a tidy sum for making his table's final two, and the prize for besting his sole remaining contender would be tidier still.

Prior to the start of the evening's play, Max and Stav had agreed that the next night's tournament would be a bridge too far. Max in particular was keen to avoid any of the suspicion which might arise from an unknown newcomer sweeping in and cleaning house two nights on the spin having only obtained membership at the casino a week earlier. Stav understood this concern without sharing it, but he had been wary that the level of skill possessed by the kind of opponents he could expect to meet in the later stages of a big-money tournament would likely minimise or even cancel out his illicit digital advantage.

But as the night wore on and Stav's hot streak continued, the lure of the big prize grew ever more prominent in both men's minds. On the rare occasions when Max had lost a hand, it had been down to plain bad luck; every single time, the face-reading aspect of the app had correctly predicted whether Stav's opponent had been holding a stronger or weaker hand than his own at the time of each bet.

Stav's final opponent, who had proven himself some combination of stronger and luckier than the rest, soon fell helplessly at his feet. Stav was announced as the night's first winner and immediately collected his winnings and joined Max at the bar.

"We have to come back tomorrow," he said, wasting no time. "A: this thing works better than we thought. And B: we just won a free buy-in. It's zero risk."

Max nodded and clinked his glass against the celebratory drink he'd ordered for Stav. "Definitely."

They spent another hour or so at the bar, with Stav doing his best to make up for Max's four-drink head start and Max doing his best to maintain his lead. When the barman gently suggested that Max should consider calling it a night, they agreed to move on to the less judgemental surroundings of the pub beneath their flat.

As Stav formally registered for the following night's big tournament, he and Max heard a commotion on the floor.

"Our second winner of the evening," an amplified male voice announced, "and our second lucky qualifier: Gary Lipton."

"No way," Stav groaned, catching a glimpse of the still-celebrating Gary Lipton. "It's *him*."

Max squinted to see what the problem was, fighting his alcohol-hit vision. "What? Who is it?"

"It's the asshole who stole your phone! The guy whose brother I beat at pool. Oh, man… they must have bought some hacked Lenses and downloaded another app to help them cheat. They found the pool app on the phone, so they know it can be done. I mean, it can't be a coincidence, right?"

"We need to get out of here right now, before he sees us," Max said, more cautious than Stav even in this inebriated state.

"I can beat him," Stav insisted. "Tomorrow night… I *will* beat him."

Max hurried outside without saying another word.

"Well?" Stav pushed, huddled over Max's computer chair.

"Nothing," Max said, quickly sobered up and now confident that no all-encompassing poker apps had been made publicly available in recent days. "He's either using the card calculator *or* the facial scanner. There's no way him or his brother would be smart enough to combine them into an app like we did."

Stav thought quietly for several seconds, seeing no need to correct Max's overly generous use of the word *we* in relation to their app's development. "And you don't think his brother could be sitting somewhere with the phone, alternating between two apps? They wouldn't exactly have to be geniuses to figure out that they could do *that*, right?"

Max leaned back in his chair and ruffled his hair. "If they're doing that, it's basically a level playing field. The only difference would be that his brother has to control the phone to keep changing between the apps, whereas I don't have to do anything since our app has both features built in."

Stav didn't like the sound of a level playing field; after all, the whole point of using the Lenses was to ensure that he had a competitive advantage over his opponents.

"I'm going to bed now, anyway," Max announced. "We'll think about everything properly in the morning."

Stav ignored these words and stared at the wall in deep thought.

Max knew this look and stood silently until Stav's mental gears stopped turning and his eyes lit up.

"That's it," Stav said. "The phone!"

"What about it?"

"It's *your* phone," Stav excitedly clarified. "They stole *your* phone."

"So?"

"So can't you do something to control or access it remotely? Through your computer or something? Because if you could do something that would let us see what Gary's Lenses pick up, we'd know exactly what cards he's holding. We literally couldn't lose."

Max shook his head; as good as this sounded, he knew there was no way. "Besides," he said, "even if they are using the same phone, they probably already wiped it."

"Nah," Stav said. "Those idiots wouldn't have been able to open up a new XK6 to all that homebrew stuff like you did. Your pool app was already on the phone so they knew it was hacked. And when they saw that, they must have bought a pair of hacked Lenses online then looked for a poker app. But obviously there *isn't* a real poker app floating around, so they settled on the separate apps for probability and face-scanning. They know it's not going to be long before everyone in Britain knows people are walking around with hacked Lenses, so they know time is tight. Anyway… that all makes more sense than anything else. Don't you think?"

Max couldn't spot any obvious holes in this logic; it certainly didn't strike him as likely that the idiot brothers would have thought it worthwhile to buy another XK6 when they had already stolen one from him.

Stav narrowed in on his idea. "Let's just say, for the sake of argument, they *are* still using your old phone. Would there — theoretically — be any way for you to see what Gary sees?"

"No," Max said, a slight grin spreading across his face. "But there is *something* I could do…"

~

One phrase encapsulated Gary Lipton's style of play more than any other: slow and steady.

Max and Stav understood that this slowness was a result of Gary's need to wait for his unseen brother to alternate between calculating probabilities and scanning his opponents' faces, but other players occasionally expressed frustration at his ponderous approach.

Stav, chip leader by a distance, watched with keen interest as Gary and the only other remaining player battled over a pot that would bring one of them within sight of Stav and the other within sight of elimination. Stav's app confidently predicted that Gary's hand was the strongest by far, so it came as little surprise when the other man eventually lost patience over Gary's overly slow play and voiced a firm but restrained complaint to the dealer.

In Stav's Lens-assisted vision, the man's face lit up with annotations and markers pointing to uncountable tiny physical manifestations of his frustration. Gary won the hand before long and the third man was eliminated within another ten minutes.

Stav and Gary stared each other down as they prepared to go head to head for the big prize. Gary, after initially looking like he'd seen a ghost when he first saw that Stav would be competing against him, had maintained an aura of confidence throughout the marathon tournament. Both knew perfectly well that the other was augmenting his skills with assistance from an app, and both were unsurprised to be left facing only the other. Stav had expected slightly stiffer competition from the rest of the field, but each successive hand proved all over again just how infallible Max's app really was.

Unlike during the previous night's qualifying tournament, Max, phone safely tucked inside his pocket, now stood in the viewing area opposite Stav's seat. When he left this area after a few back-and-forth hands, Stav knew exactly what was coming.

Max retreated to the bar and ordered a spiced rum and lemonade. While he waited, he lifted his phone from his pocket. After temporarily and necessarily ceasing communication with Stav's Lenses, Max logged into his Systelonik account. Within a few clicks, he had reported his old phone as stolen and was now faced with an enticing option:

"Securely wipe all data and disable all operations? [WARNING: Selecting this option will IMMEDIATELY AND IRREVOCABLY brick your device!]"

Max took a sip of his drink, began walking back towards the viewing area, and pressed *Yes.*

~

The look on Gary Lipton's face said it all.

His head darted around the room, as though looking for his unseen brother to ask why the hell all of the overlaid data in his vision had just disappeared.

"You alright?" Stav asked with a barely concealed smile. "You look like you've lost something."

Gary said nothing. The smirk on Stav's face told him that the data hadn't suddenly disappeared by chance, but there was nothing he could say. As Stav and Max had counted on, Gary knew better than to seek sympathy by complaining to the dealer that his opponent had somehow interfered with the app he'd been using to cheat with. Second place would win Gary a sizeable sum; enough to keep his mouth shut, if not to dull the pain of being bested by the couple of losers he'd robbed a week earlier.

Within five hands, it became apparent to Stav that Gary had no idea what he was doing and had been utterly dependent on his still-unseen brother's remote assistance. Unlike Stav, Gary hadn't even been a casual poker player before stumbling into this supposedly foolproof get-rich-quick scheme.

The rest of the observers put Gary's sudden and spectacular collapse down to mental fatigue, and most were glad that Stav's inevitable victory came mercifully quickly.

"Unlucky, mate," Stav said, taunting Gary with the offer of

a handshake as Max punched the air in delight behind him. "Maybe next time."

Gary muttered something under his breath and reluctantly shook Stav's hand. He collected his runner-up prize and made a swift exit. His brother appeared at the door, leading to angry remonstrations from Gary, who refused to accept any of the blame for falling at the last hurdle.

Max joined Stav for the presentation of the small trophy and the handover of the cash prize. The casino quickly returned to its usual Sunday night vibe, with casual players rolling dice and crossing their fingers.

When Max and Stav eventually called it a night after too many spiced-rum-and-lemonades to count, they walked outside to the waiting taxi.

"We did it," Stav said, sinking into his seat and shaking his head in disbelief. "We bloody did it!"

Max looked out of the window and smiled. "Yeah, man. We bloody did."

TWELVE

Amos

"Take a seat, Pinewood," Isaiah Amos said. "We don't have long."

On the streets beneath his 22nd floor office, a crowd had already formed around Sycamore HQ ahead of the 10am launch event for SycaStars United, a groundbreaking reality show which would — as the name suggested — unite all of the nation's most-watched and best-loved SycaStars under one roof. Those SycaStars were waiting patiently downstairs, being well looked after in some of Sycamore HQ's luxury lounges.

"As you know," he continued, "every eye is going to be on this place today. I need you to monitor the metadata on communications within the vicinity, looking for anything remotely suspicious that might hint at a planned disruption."

"Will do," Kate said. "And since you're going to be down there in the middle of it all, you're in the best place to keep an eye on the SycaStars themselves. Dangerman might try something; you know his shtick. But some of the girls could be a bigger problem if—"

"The girls? Go on..."

"Well, Damian Dangerman is Damian Dangerman... so people *expect* stupid stunts. But the girls? Some of them are really struggling. Not so much Trixilicious — she's a force of nature — but some of the others have been falling apart in the last four or five days. It's one thing being an online celebrity like they all were before The Seed, but it's a totally different thing having your entire life streamed live for the world to see. Most people just aren't built to handle that."

"So what's the danger?" Amos asked, growing impatient as the time ticked towards 10am. "You think one of them could have a breakdown on the show?"

Kate shook her head. "Well, maybe, but if someone has a breakdown during the show… fine. That's gold. I'm thinking about *today*. I don't think any of them are quite at the point where they'd speak out about how they're feeling or how dehumanising it all is. I'll look back at their logs from bathroom breaks this week, which is when they talk to their agents and helpers. That'll let me see if any of them were reluctant to do SycaStars United. Who's all going to be talking?"

"Only myself and Trixilicious have been announced to speak. There's a Q&A at the end, then a brief meet and greet, but I can quietly exclude anyone you flag up." Amos stood up and headed to his elevator. "Stay here and look into those bathroom breaks, Kate. Good thinking."

Kate, understanding not only her responsibility in ensuring the SycaStars waiting downstairs were all in a suitable frame of mind but also the trust Amos had shown by leaving her alone on his immaculate and sprawling 22nd floor, got straight to work. She scanned the automatically generated text logs of the SycaStars' private spoken conversations with their agents and handlers; fortunately for Amos, none had expressed serious reservations about the show, much less plans to sabotage its launch.

But with around ten minutes to go before the event began, Kate's regular scan of high-traffic foreign articles regarding Sycamore revealed something alarming. She wasted no time in calling Amos to alert him that Adeline Lemarchand, a French journalist who had recently caused a major political incident by leaking sensitive communications provided by an unknown source, was currently engaged in her own online Q&A ahead of what she promised would be a major revelation from Sycamore HQ.

"It says they'll be showing *'live and exclusive undercover footage from Sycamore's heartland'*," Kate said, "and that even if the revelations aren't as incredible as she knows they will be, she strongly believes that her anonymous source will reveal himself and that his identity alone will be earth-shattering."

Amos said nothing for several seconds.

"Mr Amos... did you hear me?"

"He's here," Amos replied.

"Who?"

There was another long pause. "Kurt."

"Kurt?" Kate echoed in disbelief. "Kurt *Jacobs*? But I watched his funeral! *Everyone* watched his funeral... and you were there!"

"I have reason to believe he's alive."

Kate exploded into fury, lambasting Amos for keeping this from her for so long. For his part, Amos was too concerned about what might be coming to be angry at Kate's tone. "Do you at least know where he is?" she asked.

"We know a resistance group has been operating at La Plethora, the abandoned super mall. Their base has been neutralised, but Kurt may not have been with them; and if he ever was, he may have escaped in time. It's possible they saw the scouting drones and knew something was coming. Kurt's family disappeared a few days ago, which suggests he and Terrance are alive... or at least *were* alive at that point. And, like them or not, we're dealing with smart people here."

"Understatement! If Minter is with Kurt and they're trying to take us down..." Kate let the sentence fade off. "So what kind of emergency access did Minter have to core Sycamore systems? Was there anything in place in case something happened to his Seed? Remote access or anything? If there was, you must have locked him out… right?"

Amos was quiet, realising the extent of what his Emergency Control Interface — explicitly designed to *prevent* sabotage — would allow Minter to do.

Kate took Amos's silence for what it was: a recognition that things were, in all likelihood, about to get extremely difficult. From a personal standpoint, Kate was entirely unprepared to relinquish the power she'd grown used to. She had endured a few bumps on the road, with obstructive consumers like Kayla Monroe and David Brown making her life more complicated than it had to be, but despite these complications she had quickly come to love her ability to eavesdrop on any conversation under the guise of protecting the integrity of Sycamore's systems — so much so that she had already all but abandoned her prior focus of attaining superstardom through her role as host of *This Week On Sycamore*.

"We can't give up," she said, desperate to cling on to what was hers.

"It might not be Kurt," Amos said. "Even if Lemarchand isn't bluffing and she does actually have something, the source could be anyone."

Again, Kate could read more into what Amos *didn't* say. The subtext was clear: if Adeline Lemarchand's anonymous source *did* reveal himself to be Kurt Jacobs, their time atop the ivory tower was through.

"I have to go," he went on. "We're live in two minutes. Keep an eye on everything from up there and I'll do my part down here."

At 10am, Amos played that part better than anyone else could have, smiling broadly as he introduced Trixilicious and Damian Dangerman before diving further into the details of what viewers could expect from SycaStars United. He fell back upon a well-rehearsed speech and after a few minutes felt increasingly sure that Adeline Lemarchand had been played for a fool; despite her grand promises, nothing had happened.

But then, at 10:05, everything hit the fan.

Although nothing alarming appeared in Amos's own vista, the sudden distraction all around him suggested that everyone else was seeing something. The boos and abuse which soon followed removed all doubt.

Amos gestured into his palm, trying to call Kate to ask what she could see. His Seed, and by extension his entire account, was completely unresponsive. His next attempt to deduce what was going on involved asking the heckling crowd. Predictably, he was quickly drowned out.

"Why did you call my fans oxygen thieves?" Trixilicious asked angrily.

And with that, Amos knew: there had been a leak of his own conversations. Such a leak, without doubt, could only have come from the hands of Terrance Minion and Kurt Jacobs. In comparison to what comments they could have chosen to leak, his dismissal of Star's Eye View fans as oxygen thieves — a point he privately stood by — was a surprisingly low-key choice. Perhaps *unnervingly* low-key…

Mercifully for Amos, the familiar SycaLotto jingle began to play in the ears of everyone present; if this didn't distract them, nothing would. Amos looked up to the sky like everyone else, all conditioned like Pavlov's dogs to watch the next draw. Within a few seconds of what he'd hoped would be a respite, however, he learned the true nature of this universal video placement.

Because rather than a mega jackpot SycaLotto draw, the video which played on the giant virtual screen was a short and snappy montage containing footage of Stacy Palamino's murder and Amos's brazen confession. Only "confession" wasn't quite the right word; rather than confess, he proudly took credit.

The crowd's mood soured instantly, turning from hostile to threatening in the blink of an eye. Yells of "murderer" and "animal" landed on Amos. He found himself desperately scanning the area for his security officers. With no help in sight and surrounded on three sides by what had quickly become an angry and potentially bloodthirsty mob, he turned towards Sycamore HQ's entrance and prepared to make a run for it.

As Amos focused on the glass doors, a body dashed in front of him and blocked his way. His eyes froze on the obstructor's face. The crowd fell eerily silent when they realised, at the same time as Amos, exactly who they were looking at:

Kurt Jacobs.

What the crowd had seen so far — incontrovertible evidence of Amos's involvement in Stacy Palamino's murder, as well as various pieces of demographically targeted evidence of abuses of power on a maniacal scale — had been incredible enough. But now, standing before them, they saw the well-known face of a man they had all fully believed to be dead.

Kurt spoke more loudly than he had to in the silence, warning Amos to think before he acted since everything he did was currently being streamed live on international television.

It felt to Isaiah Amos as though the rug had been pulled out from underneath him by none other than the man who designed it; the cruelest irony, of course, was that the very man who dreamt up the game-changing Seed was the one doing the pulling.

Amos tried to compose himself. Even in this context, when he looked at Kurt he saw a man capable of reason. "Come on, hotshot," he pleaded. "We can put this right. We can go back to how it was. Everything can go back to how it was."

There was disgust on Kurt's face and gloating in his voice as he dismissed this notion out of hand: "Nothing goes back to anything," he insisted. "We go nowhere. There is no we. You go to prison and I go home. That's what we do."

Amos no longer felt any worry or regret. His anger left no room for anything else. He fumed at Kurt and the heckling crowd, lambasting their ungratefulness for all he had done. "I gave you all everything," he yelled, "and what do I get?"

A small but sharp rock crashed into his head.

"That's what you get!" its thrower jibed. Mass laughter ensued.

As Amos nursed his head, a member of the crowd leapt over the security barrier and wasted no time in smashing a hole in Sycamore HQ's glass facade. He encouraged others to follow; without hesitation, they did. A swarm soon flooded inside.

Frightened staff, ignored by the angry but largely non-violent ransackers, began to flee. Amos viewed this as an unforgivable dereliction of duty but was smart enough to realise that he would never get a chance to punish the cowards; in light of the explosive truths Kurt and Terrance were in the process of revealing, Amos knew that his position at Sycamore — and, indeed, the position of Sycamore itself — was utterly untenable.

The building was entirely overrun within minutes. Damian Dangerman had already joined the mass of pillagers and urged his many fans in the crowd to follow.

Amos tried to warn Kate to get out of his office, which was publicly known to be on the grand building's 22nd floor and would likely be a prime target for Damian and his mob. His Seed remained unresponsive, and a small pop-up notification now appeared:

Account terminated.

~

As Damian Dangerman and an overloaded mass of humanity ascended in one of Sycamore HQ's elevators, Kate Pinewood stood nervously by the window. Upon seeing Damian encourage more members of the crowd to storm the building, she had opened a small window within her vista which relayed Damian's vision. She knew he had pressed 22. She knew he was coming.

"Hey, you!" Damian said, beaming as he emerged from the elevator. He raised a hand to the crowd behind him, holding them off. "Kate Pinewood, right? Don't worry, no one is going to hurt you."

Kate didn't say anything.

Damian pointed forwards, causing his followers to flood past and begin overturning several of the sofas strewn across the floor of Amos's ostentatious office. "Someone help me toss this one out," he said. More volunteers than necessary stepped forward and assisted Damian in throwing a sofa through the window, sending it crashing to the ground below. He turned to Kate. "Put *that* on your show."

"Uh, I don't think the show will—"

Already halfway to the elevator, Damian cut off Kate's reply with another order to his obedient mob. "Upstairs! I want to find that creepy-ass wall where they spy on our vistas."

Kate sat on the nearest intact and right-way-round sofa, overwhelmed by the whole situation. She scanned for vistas with the best views of Amos and Kurt and picked a well-behaved consumer standing just a few metres away.

She could see shards of glass falling to the ground as Damian's wrecking squad smashed more windows upstairs. A voice called for Kurt to get out of there but he stayed for a few more seconds.

"You're going to get killed," he yelled at Amos, who was perilously close to a lot of the falling debris.

Amos shrugged, feigning indifference. Kate knew him well enough to recognise how hollow this was, and she imagined Kurt did too. The expression on Amos's face was far from stoic; more stunned than defiant. His body, likewise, was more frozen to the spot in disbelief than engaged in a symbolic last stand.

The same voice as before called out to Kurt: "Seriously, Kurt: forget him. Come on!"

From the 22nd floor of Sycamore's crumbling HQ, Kate Pinewood used her unchecked eavesdropping powers to watch from relative safety as Kurt Jacobs looked at Isaiah Amos one final time.

"You lose," Kurt said, and Amos's game was over.

Author's Notes

Thanks for reading *Sycamore XL*

If you enjoyed this collection, it would be incredibly helpful if you could spare a few moments to leave a review on Amazon.

Thank you — I greatly appreciate it.

A message to long-time Sycamore fans

There would have been no *Sycamore 2,* no *Sycamore X* and no *Sycamore XL* if early readers of the original *Sycamore* hadn't given it a chance back in 2013 and 2014 when it was my only published book, so I'd like to extend my particular and heartfelt thanks to those who have followed the series over the years.

Latest News

To receive updates on my upcoming books, you can **sign up to my author newsletter.**

To reach me directly, discuss anything related to my books, keep up to date with what's coming next and even have a chance to read some of my work before it goes public, you can also **join my Facebook fan group**.

Links to my join email newsletter and Facebook group can be found at **craigafalconer.com**

~

Not Alone

For those of you who haven't read any of my other novels yet, my top recommendation is to start with ***Not Alone*** — an international multi-format bestseller with well over 130,000 copies sold.

Not Alone is available now at Amazon and Audible, as are its sequels.

~

www.craigafalconer.com

Books by Craig A. Falconer

Not Alone: First Encounter (Prequel)

Not Alone

Not Alone: Second Contact

Not Alone: The Final Call

~ Contact Trilogy box set ~

Not Alone: Fractured Union

Not Alone: Leap of Destiny

Not Alone: Revelations

~ Discovery Trilogy box set ~

Not Alone: The Awakening

Not Alone: Hidden Wonder

Not Alone: Endgame

~ Evolution Trilogy box set ~

Not Alone: Origins

Terradox

The Fall of Terradox

Terradox Reborn

Terradox Beyond

~ Terradox Quadrilogy box set ~

Sycamore

Sycamore 2

Sycamore X

Sycamore XL

~ Cyber Seed Compendium box set (2022) ~

Sci-Fi Sizzlers

Wanderlust

Pamela 2.0

Sunset Stays

Pumpkin Splice

Happy, Inc.

When Santa Slays

Arise With Us

Replica

Whence They Came

A Scent Of Man

Megaton Murphy

Yester Year

Too Good To Be True

Bound For Glory

Funscreen

For more information, visit

www.craigafalconer.com

Printed in Great Britain
by Amazon

80464746R00082